WHEN THE EARTH WALKS...

On the lip of the smoking fissure known as the Sacred Hoofprint the Witchmen's trap was at last sprung. A small charge exploded, hurling a barrel-sized charge into the fissure. Far it fell, deeper and deeper into the very bowels of the uneasy mountain. And then, unheard by living ear, the charge exploded.

Many leagues away, Bili Morguhn felt a sudden, terrible uneasiness. And when a living carpet of small, scuttling beasts broke out of the woods to rocket downslope over the edge of the plateau, Bili let his instinct guide him. "Mount!" he roared, and had barely followed his own orders when the very earth began to shudder.

"That way!" Bili shouted, pointing to where the animals had disappeared. And as trees crashed around them and boulders shifted, slid, and tumbled, the column sped after Bili in a desperate race to escape the plateau before the entire rocky face dissolved, devouring them in its fall. . . .

More Science Fiction from SIGNET

THE
SAVAGE
MOUNTAINS

A Horseclans Novel

by
Robert Adams

Ø
A SIGNET BOOK
NEW AMERICAN LIBRARY
TIMES MIRROR

NAL BOOKS ARE ALSO AVAILABLE AT DISCOUNTS IN BULK
QUANTITY FOR INDUSTRIAL OR SALES-PROMOTIONAL USE.
FOR DETAILS, WRITE TO PREMIUM MARKETING DIVISION,
NEW AMERICAN LIBRARY, INC., 1633 BROADWAY, NEW
YORK, NEW YORK 10019.

SIGNET TRADEMARK REG. U.S. PAT. OFF. AND FOREIGN COUNTRIES
REGISTERED TRADEMARK—MARCA REGISTRADA
HECHO EN CHICAGO, U.S.A.

SIGNET, SIGNET CLASSICS, MENTOR, PLUME AND MERIDIAN BOOKS
are published by The New American Library, Inc.,
1633 Broadway, New York, New York 10019

FIRST PRINTING, JANUARY, 1980

1 2 3 4 5 6 7 8 9

PRINTED IN THE UNITED STATES OF AMERICA

For Philip José Farmer,
for Andrew J. Offutt,
and for L. Sprague and
Catherine De Camp.

For George MacCaulay
For Joe Rosenberger
For the members of NYSFS

Most important, for
Mrs. Elnora Adams, my mother.

Death rides all in plate and His tall horse is black.
　　He leads every charge and His bowstring's never slack.
He stalks every camp, He rides every raid.
　　His steel harvests warrior and merchant and maid.
Death rides a tall, black horse and we all are sworn to
　　　　　　　　　　　　　　His service.
　　A Freefighter rides for Blood and Death.
　　　　　　　　　　　　—ancient Freefighter song

THE
SAVAGE
MOUNTAINS

PROLOGUE

The narrow, winding streets of the city were dark and utterly deserted, save for the solitary figure whose worn, oft-patched boots crunched through the fresh-fallen snow. The fine stuff of the hooded cloak which shrouded the walker had commenced to fray in places, but still was thick and warm. The scabbard of a broadsword jutted out at the hooded one's side, though of all the folk still alive within the walls of the doomed city, he was the man least likely to be attacked.

Not that *Vahrohneeskos* Drehkos Daiviz of Morguhnpolis was universally loved. There were full many who actively hated the short, stocky, middle-aged nobleman, especially among the more religious elements of the population. But there was not a man or woman who would have dared to lift hand against him who commanded the city and its defense, for, harsh and uncompromising as had been his tenure, but few of his schemes and strategems had failed, while each and every one of his predictions had inexorably come to pass.

Most of those few thousands remaining in besieged Vawnpolis were common people—peasant villagers of this Duchy of Vawn and its neighboring principality, the Duchy of Morguhn; Vawnpolee and Morguhnpolee city dwellers, servant-class types, miners, herders and the like—and all were deeply riddled with superstitition, else they would never have become involved in the insanity which had brought them to these sorry straits.

Inflamed by the *kooreeeoee* and priests, who had been abetted by a handful of minor nobles, they had schemed and plotted against their rightful lords and finally had risen up and murdered many of them. In Vawn, the rebellion had been an unqualified success. But, due to a number of factors, in Morguhn it had failed miserably and, worse, had cost the lives not only of many Morguhn rebels but of hundreds of the Vawnee who had ridden to aid them. Of the two *kooreeooe*, Holy Skiros of Morguhn was known to have been captured by the forces of the pitiless *thoheeks* of Morguhn; Mahreeos of Vawn had simply disappeared in the maelstrom-rout of the self-proclaimed Soldiers of God, whether dead, captured or in hiding, none of his erstwhile followers could say which.

Few of the rebel nobles had survived the debacle in Morguhn, and those few had bolted to the only refuge available to them, the walled city of Vawnpolis, which had been the seat of the now extirpated *Thoheeksee* of Vawn—descendants of one of the barbarian Horseclans whose rule had been imposed upon formerly Ehleen lands for a century and a half.

Though there had been, between the defeat in Morguhn and the investment of Vawnpolis, more than adequate time for every man or woman or child of the rebels to escape, to flee before the avenging forces, there had never been a safe direction in which to flee—Morguhn lay to the east, the loyal Duchy of Skaht lay to the north and the equally loyal Duchy of Baikuh lay to the south; west lay grim death in the terrible form of wild, savage mountain tribes.

Just before harvest time, after a hotly contested march, the army now besieging Vawnpolis had arrived under its walls. Twenty thousand Confederation Regulars had marched under their cat standards, along with almost every loyal nobleman of fighting age, their relatives, retainers and companies of hired Freefighters, most of the latter being natives of the Middle Kingdoms, which lay several hundred miles to the north. This vast host—more than thirty thousand warriors, in all—was led by High Lord Milo of Morai and High Lady Aldora Linszee Treeah-Pohtohmas Pahpas, two of the Undying Triumvirate who had ruled the Confederation since its inception. Only they were aware that the rebellion, though cloaked in religious trappings, was really sparked by ageless agents of the Witch Kingdom, situated in the huge and trackless Salt Swamp of the farthest south.

With the siegelines drawn and fortified, the bulk of the nobles had been sent home to see to their harvests, while their Freefighter companies and the Regulars maintained the investiture. With the crisp air of autumn, they returned with reinforcements, swelling the total strength of the army to over forty thousand.

Since then, there had been three assaults on the city walls, all beaten off, but all exacting a high cost not only to attackers, but to the defenders, who could ill afford any manner of losses.

It was, Drehkos ruminated as he walked back to the Citadel, an impossible situation. Due principally to the senseless burnings of standing crops and slaughterings of herds during the first days of the Vawn rebellion, Vawnpolis had not ever been really well supplied with food and had lasted this long only because of the fever which had sporadically raged through the city, taking off mostly the youngest and the oldest and the sickly or wounded. Now, the last skeletal horse had been butchered, most of the hoarded stores were gone along with dogs and cats; even rats and mice were virtually extinct in Vawnpolis.

Before the outer works fell, it had sometimes been possible to filter small raiding parties through the lines to prey upon the camps or supply line of the besiegers, but recent attempts in this direction had resulted only in the gruesome return of the raiders by way of the investing army's catapults—their headless bodies splatting against the walls or into the streets.

At least there was no lack of fresh water from the three deep wells within the walls. Nor did they lack for fuel, since the miners had early on discovered a wide seam of hard coal beneath the city itself. But these were the only items they did not lack.

The refugee-rebels had fled their homes in haste, in summer, and the dearth of warm clothing, boots and blankets was crippling. The supply of arrows was running perilously low. Since the city's tannery had lain outside the walls, leather was become scarce and even the few green hides were husbanded. Even so mundane a thing as rope was become infinitely precious, and ordinary linen or cotton thread brought its lucky owner a silver *thrahkmeh* the yard.

For months now, no scrap of any hard metal had been allowed to sit idle. A round dozen master smiths were among the rebels in Vawnpolis, along with numerous apprentices and a superfluity of fuel; all that was lacking was a decent supply of war metals—steel, iron, bronze and brass.

The lack of horn and fishglue rendered the repair of bows almost an impossibility, and stringing those still usable was becoming more and more difficult as the supply of silk steadily dwindled. The few arrows they could find decent wood to produce were, of dire necessity, fletched with vellum and tipped with fire-hardened bone; also, Drehkos had encouraged experiments in scraping and otherwise processing bone in attempts to devise a substitute for horn, but the results had been, thus far, inconclusive.

If only . . . Drehkos Daiviz could but shake his weary head and sigh. This rebellion, now fast approaching its bloody, inevitable conclusion, had been pointless and wasteful, and those involved, himself included, had been fools and worse. How can an egg be unscrambled? And it would be as simple to do that as to return any part of the Confederation to its pre-Horseclans condition—Ehleen-ruled and principally Christian.

How could he and the other nobles have allowed the *kooreeooee* to so delude them? Poor Myros, at least, was more or less mad and might be excused on that ground. But the rest of them should have known better, should have known their Holy Cause was foredoomed to failure, should have realized that a mere handful of nobles and a few thousands Soldiers of Christ—ill-armed, half-trained peasants and city riffraff—had not the chance of a snowball in Hell against the professional troops they were certain to face.

As the torches at the Citadel gate glowed ahead, he consciously set his face in a smile, that those good men within might not think him either worried or displeased. For he was definitely not displeased, not with them, anyway. They—common and gentle and noble . . . yes, and even cleric—had done more, done longer and done with less than anyone had any right to expect.

And his smile broadened, involuntarily, at the swell of his fierce pride in these, *his* men. Their bravery, stoicism in suffering privations and self-sacrifice, should, by rights, have bought them their lives and guaranteed their futures; in truth, he and they would all soon be dead. He only hoped that what they had done here would be remembered by those who opposed them, even after the Holy Cause which had brought them all to this pass had been long years relegated to that dungheap from which it should never have been resurrected.

Chapter I

Although the camps scattered about the headquarters hill resounded with the raucous gaiety of the besieging army's celebration of the year-end Sun Festival, the woman and eight men gathered about the board in the commander's pavilion were subdued, drinking little and eating less. Of the ten *thoheeksee* who had led the march out of Morguhnpolis last summer, seven were left alive, but only five had been hale enough to ride to this feast, and all of them bore either bandages or new scars.

Old Sir Ehdt Gahthwahlt, Confederation siegemaster, tapped the dottle from his pipe, picked up his winecup, then set it back, untasted. "Had one of my officer-students propounded a situation of this sort, even as late as a year ago, I'd have pegged him a madman!" He snorted, feelingly. "The whole damned thing's impossible! A few thousand ill-supplied, ill-equipped, starveling wretches of amateur soldiers simply *cannot* hold the antique walls of a small hill town against four times their number of professionals—and half of that force, units of the best damned army any of us will ever see. It's completely illogical!"

Ahrkeethoheeks Lahmahnt mindspoke, while sipping thin broth through a copper tube and longingly eyeing the joints of meat—broth and milk and wine having been his only sustenance since the physician, Master Ahlee, had wired shut his shattered jaws after the most recent attack. "Logical or not, Sir Ehdt, I face the reality of it every time I shave. It might almost lead one to wonder at the power of a religion that can give its adherents what it takes to do the impossible. . . ."

Thoheeks Morguhn set down his silver winecup with a crash. The lamp flames played on his scarred, shaven scalp as he tilted back his head to vent a harsh laugh. "My lord *ahrkeethoheeks*, men sometimes die for religion, but they don't fight for religion. Men fight for blood and loot and

5

women and great captains. The rebels are fighting for
Drehkos Daiviz, not for any blood-drinking, crucified god.
When they've beaten us off, do you hear them praising
their god or his priests? Of course not! That whole city
erupts with cheers for Lord Drehkos. Should they be suddenly bereft of him, they'd fold up like an empty
wineskin."

Old *Thoheeks* Duhnkin belched twice, resoundingly,
then nodded. "Aye, Bili, I too have noted that. Ah, Sacred
Sun, but it was a bitter and cursed day when so obviously
worthy and talented a Kinsman chose to turn against his
Kindred and throw in his lot with a traitorous pack of
Ehleenee scum." He belched once more, then added, "For,
to my way of thinking, our Confederation could well use
such a gifted leader."

The High Lord, Milo Morai, who had but recently returned from his capital to rejoin the army, agreed. "Yes,
thoheeksee, never has any realm a superfluity of good
leaders. And I admit to you all, his crimes notwithstand-
ing, I could be quite magnanimous to *Vahrohneeskos*
Drehkos Daiviz of Morguhn, in the right circumstances.
And him who delivered me said baronet alive would not
go unrewarded, either. In return for the sworn services of
a Drehkos, I would even be willing to negotiate generous
terms in the surrender of Vawnpolis."

At this, several of the *thoheeksee* growled and the
young Morguhn slammed a callused palm on tabletop.
"My liege must be aware that he owns all my fealty and
devotion, but such an action would be wrong. I must tell
him so. I well recall a day last summer, in a blood-
splashed cornfield, when my lord spoke otherwise. He then
felt that, any other considerations apart, the only way to
be sure of no future rebellions was to utterly extirpate this
lot of rebels."

Milo shrugged. "Times change, Bili, as do conditions;
the wise man will alter his conduct, conceptions and plans
accordingly. A good sword is flexible and a good man,
adaptable. Admittedly, we still could probably do it your
way—batter our way into Vawnpolis, butcher its inhabitants to a man and raze the walls and structures. But such
a course is certain to be very costly, in terms of men and
in terms of money, both of which will be needed in full
measure, come spring, as will all of you and your levies.
But more of that, anon.

"With regard to Drehkos and to Sun knows how many more of these rebels, there be this: When I journeyed back to Kehnooryos Atheenahs, two months ago, it was principally for the purpose of personally conducting two very important prisoners, the so-called *Kooreeoee* Skiros of Morguhn and Mahreeos of Vawn. Arrived in the capital, these two were put to the question, with all that that implies. It was not an easy task, nor a quick one, but eventually I got the truth from them, the whole truth, much of which but reinforced what I had already known.

"And the three men—there was another *kooreeos*, captured at Gafnee, who chanced to die while being questioned by High Lady Mara, last summer—were not what they seemed. Though their minds occupied the husks of men who had really been ordained priests and confirmed *kooreeoee*, they were still imposters, intent upon creating as much havoc as possible in the Confederation. Gentlemen, those spurious *kooreeoee* were as old as I am, maybe even older! But Sacred Sun had not gifted them as the true Undying are gifted. Rather, were they of that hellish breed commonly called 'Witchmen'!"

Several of the *thoheeksee* grasped at their Sun medallions, while old Sir Ehdt and *Thoheeks* Bili Morguhn made the Sign of Sacred Steel in the air before them.

Smiling, the High Lord reassured them all, saying, "Despite what you may have heard, gentlemen, there is nothing supernatural about these, our enemies. They are highly dangerous, make no mistake, but they be no sorcerers; rather have they perverted certain disciplines of knowledge, knowledge which first saw light in the days before the death of that world which preceded this one.

"Nearly a thousand years ago, your distant ancestors—over two hundred million of them, of a vast diversity of races—dwelt in a principality which was one though it stretched from the Sea of Sun Birth to another which lies far west of the Sea of Grass. Then was the Great Salt Swamp mostly dry land, full of farms and pasturelands, cities and towns and, probably, more people than now live in all the lands of our Confederation.

"All these many people were ruled by men chosen to represent them. These men met in a great city which was almost totally destroyed, the ruins of which now lie beneath the waters of the lakes and bays near the mouth of the North River of Kehnooryos Ehlas. So rich were the people and the nation which they ruled that vast sums could be spent on various projects which had little to do with such basic needs as food production, war preparation and the like.

"One such project was the effort to transport men to the stars by means which I'll not even attempt to explain to you. An auxiliary project, part of the star-journey project, was the need to find a way of prolonging human lifespans, since even the nearer stars lay a distance of years away. The men and women assigned to search out these means were all concentrated in a highly secret place in that subprincipality which now is the Great Salt Swamp.

"Unfortunately for Sun knows how many, they were successful in their search. They found a way to prolong a given number of human minds, almost indefinitely. But intuitively realizing what the most of humanity would think of their answer to the problem, they took every precaution to conceal their 'triumph,' so that it was only bare months before the Great Catastrophe that the Congress—which is what the gathering of ruling representatives was then called—and certain newsmongers discovered just how horrible was that method.

"The outcries of the millions who had chosen those representatives was loud and long and outraged. And those rulers, who wished to remain such, quickly reacted by ordering the project to prolong life immediately canceled, all its records destroyed and its personnel discharged and widely dispersed.

"However, ere their will could be implemented, there commenced the series of events which led to the destruction of nations, races and cultures. Because of their still secret and isolated location, the couple of hundred people in the project area, which was called the Kehnehdee Research Center, survived unharmed by firerain or plagues. When the plagues had run their course, they allowed a few, pitiful outsiders to join them as 'breeding stock.'

"You see, gentlemen, what they had discovered was a way to transfer the mind and memories from an aging to a younger body—man to man, woman to woman, man to woman, woman to man and even, so I understand, man or woman to certain animals! And so they have continued their parasitic existence down through the centuries, their aged, evil minds using one young, vibrant body after another.

"And their grand design is nothing less than to make the entire world their slaves. They were ready to do it by force of arms four hundred years ago, but the earthquakes and floods, the tidal waves and the subsidence of most of the huge peninsula whereon they dwelt utterly confounded their schemes. Though most of the original parasites survived that disaster, they lost much of their carefully maintained equipment—which was irreplaceable—all save a couple of their population centers and eight of every ten of their serf-soldiers. And virtually overnight their rich, productive lands were become, at the very best, sterile for years from their drenching of seawater.

"They have not yet fully recovered. Even so, they recognize the Confederation as a menace to their eventual intent, standing united on their very border as we do. Therefore they continue to foment trouble from within and without—trying to weaken us, divide us. This rebellion, which started at Gafnee and is ending here, was their third effort against us since the coming of the Horseclans. And we must finish it quickly, even at the cost of some concessions, for we will be face to face with their fourth effort all too soon. To combat this new and awesome threat effectively, gentlemen, the Confederation will need every arm that can swing sword or pull bow!"

Sir Geros Lahvoheetos of Morguhn stood and leaned across the small table to refill his guest's winecup, a completely natural action on the part of a young man who, born of upper-servant class, had spent most of his life as a valet to noblemen.

His guest, however, slapped a horny hand on the tabletop, exclaiming in the harsh, nasal accents of Harzburk, "Now, dammit, Geros . . . ahh, *Sir* Geros . . . *that* just is not done! You're *noble*, now, man. You're a knight of Duke Bili's household, which means you outrank *me*. You *ask* if I want more wine; then, since your servant seems to have absented himself, *I* refill my own cup . . . and yours, if you so indicate."

Sinking back onto his seat, the husky, olive-skinned knight sighed and shook his shaven head. "Oh, Pawl, Pawl . . . I was so happy before, as a simple color sergeant, as merely a comrade of your troop. I never aspired to nobility. Tell me, Pawl, was I . . . did you consider me to be a good soldier, a good Freefighter?"

The silvery bristles on the guest's pate flashed in the lamplight as his head bobbed. "Sir Geros, I will always feel honored that you learned your craft under me. Yes, you were an excellent Freefighter, none better."

Sir Geros sighed once more. "Then why, Pawl? Why could they not just leave me where I was so happy? Why was it necessary to thrust nobility on me? Force me to bear a title which I will never be able to live up to? What did I do to deserve such?"

Pawl Raikuh's scarred features registered stunned dismay. "Are you daft, man, to talk so? One who did not know better would think you'd been condemned to some dire punishment. Man, in one day, you saved your lord's life, slew the biggest warrior I've ever seen *and* performed an act of bravery which, though I witnessed every moment of it, I still can hardly believe! What did you expect? A pat on the head and, maybe, a new sword?"

Geros raised his dark, troubled eyes. "I would have been more than happy with such, Pawl." His fingers toyed with the silver cat pendant on his chest. "After all, I but did what any man of the *thoheek*'s would have done during the battle, for he is a good lord and kind. As for the other, well . . ." Embarrassed, he dropped his gaze. "I still don't know why I did it, didn't really realize I *was* doing it until I found myself down there in the fire and the heat. But it's as I said, Pawl. The officer was hurt and everyone could see he would soon be burned alive. If I had not, another would've."

"Turkey dung!" snorted Raikuh. "I was *there*, Sir Geros. Remember?"

He could.

The hilltop salient had been but a trap set by the crafty leader of the rebels. The fortifications, garrisoned by suicide troops, had been undermined, supported only by oil-soaked timbers which had been secretly fired. The stratagem had failed on the twin hillock, assaulted and taken by troops under the personal command of the High Lord; his mindspeak warning had arrived barely in time for most of the Confederation forces to quit the dangerous area.

Only a single, rearguard company had been still at the periphery of the trap when it was sprung. When the dust had settled, it could be seen that but a single member of that company had survived. And he was facing a cruel, gruesome death, his legs securely pinned under a huge, smoldering timber, unable to draw his sword and his dirk missing.

Several men on the lip of the still-settling crater had attempted to throw the unfortunate officer a weapon that he might decently end his life ere the flames reached him, but the distance was too great, and *Thoheeks* Bili of Morguhn had sent a galloper to bring back an archer from the foot of the hill.

Geros could not recall all of the beginning, could not remember hastily shedding most of his armor or clambering down the crumbling slope of the crater. But he would never forget that *heat*!

It had lapped over him, enfolded him in its deadly embrace. It had savaged his flesh, set boots and clothing asmolder, made each breath a searing agony.

After an endless eternity of gingerly picking his way over an almost limitless expanse of steaming earth, jumbled stones and splintered timbers, the officer lay just before him, thanking him for his valor, asking for his dirk and urging him to return to safety.

The few moments after that were very hazy in Geros' memory . . . but in no one else's. He recalled, however, half carrying, half dragging the young officer—Captain Lehzlee, heir to *Ahrkeethoheeks* Lehzlee—to where a host of willing hands assisted them both up to safety.

But from that now cursed moment, the warm and natural comradery which he had so cherished had disappeared with the suddenness of a blown-out candle flame. The hard-bitten Freefighters, who reverenced damned few things, had seemed very uncomfortable in his presence, treating him with a deference bordering upon awe. *And he hated it all*!

Pawl Raikuh went on, "I was *there*. I saw what you did . . . though, as I said, I still scarce can credit the testimony of my own eyes. That timber was hardwood, looked to be solid oak, and near two feet thick, so it couldn't have weighed less than a ton and a half, Harzburk measure, maybe two tons. Yet you *raised* it, man! With your bare hands, you lifted near a thousand *kaiee*-weight and *held* the damned thing long enough for the captain to inch his crushed legs from under it! In my near forty years as a Freefighter, I've seen many a wonder, but if Steel allows me that many more years, I'll never again see an equal to my lord's feat in the crater—"

"*Damn it*!" Sir Geros' fist crashed onto the table, setting cups and ewer to dancing. "Damn you, Pawl Raikuh! I be nobody's *lord*, and you know it! I'm the same man I've always been, Geros Lahvoheetos, son of *Vahrohnos* Luhmahnt's majordomo. My mother was an herb gardener, who harped and sang at feasts. And I, I was a gentleman's valet, who played and sang when so ordered. It was by purest chance that I found myself thrust into the role of warrior."

Raikuh grinned. "And you took to it as naturally and easily as an otter kit swims. In short months, you were one of the best swordsmen in my troop."

"Only because I realized there was no way I could wriggle out of the situation . . . easily, and being a born coward, I wanted to stay alive. And the only way a warrior can be reasonably certain he'll survive his next battle is to make himself a master of his weapons. But I am not, can never be, as you and *Thoheeks* Bili and those reared to the Sword. I don't *like* fighting and killing, Pawl. I'll never like it.

"At least, when I was simply a Freefighter, I had the solace that when the rebellion was crushed, I'd be able to return to being what I had always been. But now, since they did these unwarranted things to me, I'll be expected to swing Steel the rest of my life and to rear any sons I happen to sire to pursue like lives.

"I say again, Pawl, I am no one's lord. Rather am I a slave in detested bondage to an undeserved reputation, an unwanted title, a silver bauble and a couple of feet of sharp steel."

A feeling of fatherliness swept over the fiftyish captain. He reached across the table to pat Geros' clenched fist lightly. "Son, you'll not feel so in a year. Others have been similarly upset by the sudden grant of nobility . . . I've seen such. As for being no one's lord, that same year will put the lie to that statement, I'll warrant."

"Now what is that cryptic comment supposed to mean?" snapped Geros.

Tracing designs in a puddle of spilled wine and regarding the new noble from beneath bushy brows, Raikuh spoke slowly. "Why just this, Geros. Duke Bili is not so mean as to give a faithful man rank without maintenance. Your present title is but a military one, and as certain sure as steel cuts to bone, you'll be at least a *vahrohneeskos* of

Morguhn—with a fine town and croplands and kine—by this time next year, mark my words. Nor be that all, I trow. . . ."

Raising cup to lips, he took a long draught of the fine, strong wine, then continued. "That fiesty little bastard *Thoheeks* Hwahltuh of Vawn be proud as a solid-gold hilt, and he'll not forsake an opportunity like this. After all, he can truthfully attest that your deeds were done in his service, too, since we all are fighting on what are his lands. And don't you forget the House of Lehzlee, either. There be no richer or prouder house in the south of Karaleenos than Lehzlee, and you saved the life—at great personal risk—of the man who will one day be archduke and chief of that house. They're not likely to let such go unrewarded."

Geros' mind reeled. He had not even considered these possibilities. "But . . . but, Pawl, what will I do? I know nothing of farming."

Raikuh chuckled. "Damned few nobles do, son Geros. You'll do what they all do, of course. You'll find and hire a competent provost and a few overseers and a score or so over-age Freefighters to see the peace be kept. Then you'll spend your days riding and hunting and begetting. You'll sit in judgment in your town on market days, meet in council with your overlord and peers once each moon and ride with them once each year to the archduchy council, where you will deliver up your taxes for the previous year to the High Lord's deputy.

"And someday, Geros, when you're a fat forty-odd, and your mind is filled with worry about the weather and the crops and outfitting your sons for the army and dowering your daughters well, then . . . mayhap, then, you'll think on this eve. Think how foolishly you then thought, wished to once more be back with the Morguhn troop, swinging steel and taking blows as light-heartedly as you did twenty years before."

Ere Geros could frame an answer, his big servant, Sahndos, entered, ushering in one of Raikuh's lieutenants, Krahndahl. The junior officer slapped gauntlet to breastplate in salute and announced, "My lord Geros, captain, Duke Bili summons all his nobles and officers to his pavilion, immediately, if you please."

Chapter II

"And so, gentlemen," the grave-faced young *thoheeks* soberly concluded, "we may, even now, be proceeding on borrowed time. Winter has ever been the favorite raiding season of the mountain folk, so the first blow could fall at any moment anywhere along more than five hundred miles of borderlands. That is why ending this siege quickly is so imperative."

"But Sun and Wind, Bili," burst out old *Komees* Hari Daiviz of Morguhn, "to grant *amnesty* to my no-good brother and the rest of those treacherous, murdering swine? Whose harebrained idea was that?"

"The High Lord's!" snapped the Morguhn. "Present your objections to him, if you wish, Hari. But, I warn you, mine own did scant good, nor did those of the Duhnkin or the *ahrkeethoheeks*."

Ever the apologist in all matters concerning the Confederation he had so long served, retired *Strahteegos Komees* Djeen Morguhn, the *thoheeks'* sixtyish cousin-german, nodded sagely, stated stiffly, "My lord *thoheeks*, the High Lord dare not concern himself with but this single, relatively unimportant facet of the overall problem. You see, the entire Confederation be his responsibility. I like pardoning known backstabbers no better than Hari, but I also can appreciate Lord Milo's position."

Vahrohnos Spiros Morguhn, Bili's second cousin, gingerly shifted on the padded litter which had conveyed him here, finally reaching down with both hands to ease his splinted and bandaged left leg into a more comfortable position. "But, dammit, Bili, how can we be expected to go traipsing off on a campaign into the mountains, or wherever, leaving our lands filled with unrepentant rebels and a batch of bloodthirsty priests? You've seen, the High Lord has seen, we all have seen what they did to Vawn. By mȳ steel, they'll not do the like to Morguhn!"

14

"They'll not get a chance to." Bili shook his head. "It's been decided that most of the rebel fighting men will be dragooned into the campaign force; dribbled out, a few to this unit, a few to that. The amnesty is to exclude the priests and monks; those bastards will spend the length of the campaign enjoying the comforts provided by our Morguhnpolis prison.

"Noncombatants in Vawnpolis will remain there, as will a garrison of our troops. The city will be base supply for operations immediately west of Vawn."

Pawl Raikuh sighed. "Fortunes of war, I suppose. All us Freefighters had been hopefully anticipating an intaking, a sack, a bit of booty, some old-fashioned rapine. Well, there'll be other wars . . . for some."

"How will we get word to the rebels that we now wish to treat?" This from Djaik Morguhn, Bili's younger brother—war-trained, like Bili and all his other brothers, in the Middle Kingdoms; acknowledged, despite his bare fifteen years, as one of the three best swordsmen in all the besieging army.

Vahrohneeskos Ahndros Theftehros of Morguhn was but distantly related to Bili, actually being more closely related to certain of the rebels, but, like *Komees* Djeen, he was a former Confederation Army officer . . . also, he was in love with one of Bili's widowed mothers. Nonetheless, he had been occasionally sullen since, disregarding his advices and wishes, Bili and the High Lord had seen fit to honor and enoble his former servant, Geros.

Smoothing back a lock of his raven's-wing hair with a languid gesture, he put in, "Yes, Bili, there is that factor, too. We have been anything but cordial in our responses to the two or three peace overtures the rebels have made. If, during the High Lord's absence, you and the High Lady had seen fit to heed the expert advice which *Komees* Djeen and I proffered you . . ."

Tried to ram down our throats, thought Bili, who sometimes of late had had to forcefully remind himself that this supercilious man had sat his horse knee to knee with him and the High Lord last summer at the Forest Bridge, and had suffered grievous wounds in his behalf. Ever since the *vahrohneeskos* had recovered sufficiently to join the army before Vawnpolis, he had been a divisive element among the nobles of Morguhn, immediately taking the part of any who opposed the young *thoheeks* and offering his own opposition when none other arose.

"Kinsman," said Bili, with as much forebearance and patience as he could muster, "none of us could have known that affairs would so arrange themselves, and it was the High Lord himself who rejected the first effort of the rebels to parley, ere the siege had even commenced. Him it was who first declared that we were to neither give nor ask quarter—"

"*Untrue!*" snapped Ahndros coldly. "To the extent, at least, that it was you, with your barbaric, blood-hungry, northern notions of conduct, who put the idea into the High Lord's head."

Bili shook his shaven poll bewilderedly. "Kinsman, I am afraid that you credit me with far more influence over the affairs of the mighty than ever I have owned . . . or wished to own."

"Have you not, my lord?" Ahndros sneered. "Did not the High Lord, on the morning which saw the breaking of the siege of your hall, allow you first to throw a childish temper tantrum and publicly, brutally, humiliate *Komees* Djeen, when he sagely advised you to await the arrival of Confederation Cavalry ere you pursued the rebels? Did not the High Lord then accompany you on that pursuit, riding as but another nobleman under *your* command?"

"*That* was the High Lord's expressed desire, *vahrohneeskos*," growled Bili, fighting to control the temper he could feel beginning to fray under the continued insult and insubordination.

"Then what of that morning's butchery, eh?" Ahndros prodded on. "Why, even the barbarian mercenaries, on whom you so dote, call those miles of massacre 'The Bloody Ride'! The High Lord *I* knew, with whom and under whom I served for so many years, would never have countenanced such inexcusable savageries."

The knuckles stood out whitely on Bili's clenched fists and he grated his reply from between tight-locked teeth. "Lord Ahndros, I owe *you* no explanation of my conduct or of the High Lord's. You forget your place and station, and you sorely try my patience. Nonetheless, I will tell you this much: I believe that the scope and the suddenness of the rebellion, the depth of the depravaties of the rebels, shocked the High Lord to his very core. On that morning, he admonished me to put down the Morguhn rebels in the manner of Harzburk, deal with them as would the Iron King, under whose tutelage I served more than half my life."

Ahndros either failed to notice or chose to ignore the young *thoheek's* rising rage. "And you took Lord Milo at his word, didn't you? You did it up brown! No unwashed, stinking, illiterate, barbarian burk lord could have been more callously thorough. Not only did you and your howling savages chase down and slay hundreds of fleeing men, many of them completely unarmed, that terrible morning, but you hunted the poor bastards for weeks, hunted them as if they had been beasts, dangerous vermin."

Spiros Morguhn turned himself enough to see Ahndros, grimacing with the pain of the effort. "Dangerous vermin, is it, Ahndee? Yes, I consider that an apt simile for treacherous, backbiting dogs who turn on masters. I, too, took a most willing part in that hunt. Are you going to name me a burk barbarian, too? And I agree with Bili, you've far overstepped yourself . . . for some little time now."

Komees Djeen clashed the brass hook which had replaced the missing hand on his left wrist loudly against his thigh plate, and his single, blue eye flashed fire as he came to Ahndros' defense. "I think me not, Spiros. Ahndee is but stating truths which long have needed airing.

"As I affirmed in the very beginning, that pursuit from Morguhn Hall was a senseless and savage vanity of our young and vastly inexperienced *thoheeks*. And what followed the reoccupation of deserted Morguhnpolis was inexcusable, on any grounds.

"Why, man, the Duchy of Morguhn lies more than half depopulated. Whole villages were burned to the ground, after being plundered by the arsonists. There are damned few living common women who are not well-raped widows, damned few Morguhn trees that don't dangle the rotting carcass of some poor, misled peasant pikeman.

"You all know that I . . . uhh, had my differences with our late *thoheeks*. But Hwahruhn, at least, was loved and respected by all his folk. Bili, his son, will never own anything save their fear and hate."

Bili smiled humorlessly. "Regrettably, my late father was often ill and almost always weak-willed, *Komees* Djeen. As you have learned, I am neither. If love and respect bred this damned rebellion, I can well do without both.

"As regards the 'airing of truths," had not you and the *vahrohneeskos* so well served me and the Confederation, of late, I might think you both closet rebels, such is your concern for the gentle treatment and welfare of traitors."

"Why, you arrogant young whelp!" The white-haired nobleman sprang to his feet, his hand going to his swordhilt. "I was serving the Confederation when you were being given suck! How *dare* you question my loyalty . . . or that of Ahndee, who is a better man than ever you'll be!"

Dark, slender Djaik Morguhn sidled himself to block the direct path between his brother and the furious *komees*. Nor was he the only one in the pavilion to have risen. Vaskos Daiviz, son and heir of *Komees* Hari, stood fingering the pommel of his broadsword; so, too, did all three Freefighter officers . . . and Sir Geros.

Arising suddenly, old *Komees* Hari Daiviz slapped his son's hand from proximity to his hilt and strode purposefully toward the dais, his rolling gait bespeaking the percentage of his fifty-odd years spent on the back of a horse.

"Now, by Sun and Wind, *gentlemen*, I never thought me to live to see my own kindred, the nobility of Morguhn, brawling like drunken Ehleenee trollops and pimps!

"Djaik Morguhn, resume your seat, please. Your brother stands in no danger. Djeen, if you draw that blade, you'll be needing a hook for the other hand, as well . . . and you have known me long enough to know I mean it."

"Damn it, Hari!" the one-eyed *komees* burst out petulantly. "You heard what this young whippersnapper said about me and Ahndee! And we've the right to be heard!"

"Just shut up and sit down!" *Komees* Hari snapped impatiently. "You've said more than enough already."

Ahndros opened his mouth, but *Komees* Hari spotted the movement from the corner of his eye and whirled on the *vahrohneeskos*, barking, "So, too, have you, Ahndee. This be a war council, not a Thirds Meeting. You, all of us, are here to receive our chief's orders, to advise him *if he requests such*. And I've heard no request.

"Now, I don't much cotton to the idea of granting amnesty to rebel dogs, but the High Lord has no choice; that much is plain as horse turds on snow. Nor have any of us any choice, gentlemen. The High Lord has given his orders to his *thoheeksee*; our own *thoheeks* and chief has dutifully transmitted those orders to us. It be our sworn and rightful duty to learn how best we can obey, not launch yet another senseless round of who-struck-Djahn to the point where tempers rise and swords come clear. We all be supposedly responsible, adult noblemen and officers. Let us act the parts, eh?"

He turned to Bili and offered formal salute of clansman to chief. "What would you of my son and me, Bili?"

Drehkos Daiviz did not really begin to believe it until the third message arrow was brought to him. Carefully, he unrolled the vellum bound behind the hollow brass head, smooth it out and laid it beside the two others on his cluttered desktop. The three were identical, obviously written by the same hand.

In Modern Ehleeneekos, they read:

"Milos Morai, High Lord of the Confederation of Southern Peoples, sends greetings to *Vahroneeskos* Drehkos Daiviz of Morguhn. The High Lord would confer with said *vahrohneeskos*, at his earliest convenience, that conditions may be agreed upon for the honorable capitulation of the garrison, inhabitants and city of Vawnpolis. Penned under the direction of the High Lord by Pehtros Makintahsh, Adjutant. Signed: *Milos Morai.*"

Drehkos rested his head between his hands, his bare elbows on the desk, protruding through his well-worn shirt. Furiously, he massaged his gray-shot temples, then opened his eyes and read the message through again . . . and yet again. And still it was as a dream.

This was exactly what he had promised his ragtag garrison, never for a moment deluding himself that such would ever truly come to pass. He had felt himself and every other soul within Vawnpolis irrevocably doomed and the rejections of his three attempts to treat, combined with the besiegers' steadfast refusal to suffer prisoners to live, had but reinforced his conviction. Nonetheless, he had dangled the carrot of hope before his starveling ragamuffins. Over and over, he had assured them that, could they but cost the besiegers enough losses and hold out until planting time, terms would surely be granted to spare at least the lives of the common folk.

And now the impossible dream was become fact . . . hard fact.

As the first rays of the rising sun illumined the small,

spartan room, the *vahrohneeskos'* servant entered to find his master slumped over the desk, his body racked with heaving sobs.

Drehkos arrived at the pavilion of the High Lord attended only by a pair of commoner-officers, all three of them astride guardsmen's horses, escorted by *Keeleeohstos* Sahndros Druhmuhnd, commander of the High Lord's horseguards. Inside the brazier-heated pavilion, the rebels were led to where the High Lord, the High Lady Aldora and *Ahrkeethoheeks* Lahmahnt sat ranged behind a heavy table.

After saluting, the *keeleeohstos* gruffly reported, "My Lord Milo, here be *Vahrohneeskos* Drehkos Daiviz of Morguhn. The other two rebels be commoner-officers of the *vahrohneeskos'*. Would my lord be wanting guards within?"

Milo slowly shook his head. "No need, good Sahndros. Go back and find yourself a brazier and a tipple. I'll mindcall when and if I want you."

From the moment he had been ushered in, Drehkos had stood open-mouthed, staring at the lean, saturnine figure of the High Lord. As the *keeleeohstos* clanked out, the rebel leader suddenly exclaimed, "But . . . what witchery be this? You . . . you be the bard . . . Klairuhnz, wasn't it? I had wine with you at . . . at my brother's hall last spring, before any of this unpleasantness commenced."

A smile flitted briefly across Milo's lips. "I had reason, then, Lord Drehkos, for concealing my identity. A traveling bard is always welcome in village or city or hall, among Kindred or Ehleenee. So, can you think of a better guise?"

Before Drehkos could frame an answer, Milo's smile vanished and his voice cooled and hardened. "But we are not met to discuss the past, *vahrohneeskos.* Where are your other two nobles, *Vahrohnos* Myros Deskahti of Morguhn and *Vahrohneeskos* Kahzos Boorsohthehpsees of Vawn? I had thought that you would bring them to this gathering."

"My lord," replied Drehkos, "I am empowered to speak for all, noble or common, within Vawnpolis. I left poor Kahzos in command of the city, since unhealed wounds have rendered him incapable of sitting a horse."

"And Myros?" prodded Aldora. "Is that thieving murderer also wounded . . . I hope?"

"No," Drehkos answered. "Even during the assaults, I have been loath to allow Lord Myros within proximity to weapons, for more and more frequently he lapses into violent and completely pointless rages; indeed, I have found it necessary to detail an officer and a squad to . . . to look after him."

Milo nodded once, then turned to Aldora. "It's as I said years back, my dear. The reason I opposed executing him. The man's mad, always has been, and whatever drugs that so-called *kooreeos* fed him have obviously worsened his condition."

Drehkos looked from one to the other in bewilderment. "My lord, my lady, I confess I don't understand. Drugs?"

"Just so, *vahrohneeskos*, drugs." Milo gestured at the empty chairs opposite him. "But it's a long tale. You and your officers sit down and help yourselves to the wine."

Before seating himself, Drehkos spoke with crisp formality. "My lords, my lady, please allow me to introduce my officers." At Milo's nod, he went on. "On my right stands Captain Pehtros Naimos, commander of the north wall; on my left, Captain Djaimz Trohahnos, commander of the east wall. They are not of noble birth and they are . . . ahh, have been your enemies, but they have been unswervingly faithful to me, and I have never met men who more truly epitomize the word 'gentlemen.' "

Aldora watched the two officers, saw the younger, fair-skinned Djaimz Trohahnos flush red at the unexpected public praise. This man obviously had some measure of mindspeak ability, for his mindshield was impenetrable, even in his embarrassment. The other, dark, middle-aged Pehtros Naimos, was completely unshielded and his mind literally oozed devotion to his leader.

Next, the High Lady turned her attention to Drehkos. The rebel leader bore a quite striking resemblance to Hari and Vaskos Daiviz, his brother and nephew, respectively—most of his thinning hair was white, but this was the only indication of his age; otherwise, all five and a half feet of his big-boned, wide-shouldered body looked lean and hard and fit. His helm had left a dent in his high forehead, and beneath it his eyes were bloodshot and dark-ringed with lack of sleep, his face lined with worry and care. But, withal, he was still a handsome man.

Aldora sent her mind questing forth, recoiled in shocked surprise, immediately beamed to Milo on a mindspeak level unattainable to most. "I thought you said this rebel lordling had no mindspeak."

"So everyone, all his relatives and former friends, assured me," the High Lord replied on the same level. "Why? Has he a shield?"

"Try him and see."

"Whew!" Milo tried to mask the amazement from his face. "It's like running headlong into a brick wall, isn't it?"

"It's the conscious shield of a very powerful mind, Milo," she assured him. "Yours is that strong, and so is Mara's, but I've never met another such. Not even dear old Hari Kruhguh's mind had such a formidable defense."

As is true of mindspeak "conversations," these exchanges had taken bare microseconds.

Aloud, Milo smiled again, saying, "Very well, Lord Drehkos. I believe you know *Ahrkeethoheeks* Lahmahnt, of old. On my right sits the Undying High Lady, Aldora Linsee Treeah-Pohtohmas Pahpahs."

Aldora inclined her small head slightly, the light of the lamps picking out bluish highlights in her long black hair. But beneath her slender brows, her almond-shaped black eyes never ceased their careful scrutiny of Drehkos.

"Do we all mindspeak?" asked Milo as soon as all goblets were full.

The older officer shook his raggedly barbered head. "No, my lord, I be almost *kath-ahrohs*, and my kind lack such heathenish . . . ahh, such talents."

Milo smiled. "Captain, both the High Ladies—my wife, Mara, and Aldora, here—be true *kath-ahrohsee*, yet they pose high degrees of mindspeak ability. Kindred heritage, or the lack of it, is not the determinant factor in whether a man can or cannot mindspeak. Nor are we Undying and Kindred unique, as you should very well know. Large numbers of your own Ehleenee nobles and commoners are mindspeakers, the *Vahrohnos* Myros Deskati of Morguhn amongst them."

He looked down the table at the younger officer. "And what of you, Captain Trohahnos?"

The red-haired officer squirmed, uncomfortable to be seated in the presence of such high nobility. "A . . . a little, my . . . my lord. Papa didn' mindspeak an' . . . an' Mama died 'fore she could . . . could teach me much, an' . . ."

"And you, Lord Drehkos?" inquired Milo in a voice smooth as warm honey, guileless as the coo of a dove.

The rebel lord rolled his goblet slowly between his big, scarred, weather-browned hands for a moment, then raised his eyes, grinning. "For most of my mispent life, my lord, I thought that I totally lacked that ability . . . along with many another. But last spring, when we were battling our way through the mountains, I discovered that either I had acquired it almost overnight or I'd had it all along. Yes, I do mindspeak."

"You were *in* the western mountains, man? *When*? *Where*? *Why*?" demanded Milo, leaning across the table, his fists clenched, his voice and manner now intense.

Despite his obvious puzzlement, Drehkos freely answered. "Yes, my lord, I—rather, those of us who escaped from Morguhnpolis after the rout under the walls of Morguhn Hall along with a contingent of Vawnee cavalry— circled through the mountains to get to Vawnpolis. As to where, we crossed the river into the Duchy of Skaht at Bloody Ford, rested for a few days at the old, deserted border fort, then rode west, through Raider Gap, and angled south. Or tried to."

He shuddered strongly. "If I never again hear another Ahrmehnee war-screech, it will be centuries too soon, my lord. It was a running battle every day, and nights as well, sometimes. They reverence the moon, you know, and won't fight on nights when it is in the sky. Fortunately, almost the entire hellish journey was made in clear, cloudless weather. Even so, I left nearly a third of my poor, brave fellows dead in those damned mountains!"

The High Lord's brows rose sharply and he regarded the *vahrohneeskos* with a new measure of respect. "And you won through to Vawn then. You're to be congratulated on that feat, Lord Drehkos. You apparently don't recognize just how lucky you were. Why, man, in the long-ago campaign which won Vawn and Skaht and Baikuh lands for the Confederation, whole battalions of professional soldiers were wiped out to the last man by those Ahrmehnee. The fact that you took a mounted column through the very heart of their territory and got out at all is remarkable; that you lost so few men is near miraculous.

"And your brother insisted you'd never soldiered. So,

where did you learn cavalry tactics?" He gave another tight smile. "Or siegecraft?"

Drehkos shrugged tiredly. "In the mountains, I but did what seemed right to me, what seemed the best way of extricating my command from our various difficulties and predicaments. Hari was being candid with you, my lord; I never had soldiered prior to my involvement in this . . . this insanity."

He sat back and met the High Lord's gaze squarely. "I won through the mountains only because the men who accompanied me were the best and the bravest these lands have ever known. Both Pehtros and Djaimz, here, were among them. Of the rest, alas, far too many are since slain in this beastly, senseless prolongation of what was a lost cause before its inception.

"As regards my defense of the city, I discovered some ancient books within the Citadel and applied certain of their contents to the problems confronting me when the overall command of Vawnpolis was thrust onto my shoulders."

All at once, he dropped his gaze to the brilliant carpet. "I still do not know why I ever agreed to take part in this stupid foolishness. I can but ascribe it to a temporary insanity engendered by the loss of my dear wife and the ensuing loneliness, for ever have I considered warfare a monumental stupidity. Nor did I truly crave to possess my brother's lands and title."

He straightened then and once more met the High Lord's eyes. "My lords, my lady, I offer those words not as excuse, only as explanation . . . as best I, myself, can understand. Lord Sahndros, my officers and I, all of us admit our crimes and are ready and willing to submit to appropriate dooms, but only on the ironclad condition that our soldiers and the noncombatants within Vawnpolis be spared their lives, and their few meager possessions and be quickly furnished food. As for poor, sick Myros, I cannot answer, but I think my lord must agree that it were pointless to slay a madman for his actions, no matter how heinous."

Drehkos arose and the two officers quickly followed suit. "I am prepared to surrender my person to you now, my lords, if you agree to my stipulations."

Milo shook his head curtly. "But I do not agree, *vahrohneeskos*. Sit down."

Slowly, Drehkos sank back into his chair. Of course, he had known from the beginning that his position was not sufficiently strong to allow him to dictate the terms of the capitulation . . . but he had had his hopes, now dashed. His face and bearing mirrored his disappointment.

The High Lord once more leaned across the table. "Are any of you three Initiates of the Inner Mysteries of the Faith?"

The two officers just shook their heads, and Drehkos replied, "No, my lord, there never were very many of them, and only the *kooreeoee* who initiated them and their fellow initiates ever knew them. For some reason, I was never approached, nor, I think, was Lord Kahzos."

"Then," said the High Lord, "you may thank whatever gods may be for your good fortune. My offer for the capitulation of Vawnpolis is full pardon and amnesty to all within its walls, saving only priests, monks and those laymen who are Initiates of the Inner Mysteries. Think you my offer fair and acceptable, Lord Drehkos?"

Drehkos could not speak, could not move, could hardly even think or breathe. At the very best he had expected for himself and his immediate subordinates a lengthy period of suffering and humiliation followed by a painful death; at worst, he had seen a continuation of the agonies of the siege until the city eventually fell by storm and/or starvation, with all the horrors of a sack to be visited upon the survivors of that last battle.

Pardons and amnesties had never even entered his suppositions, not for himself and the surviving layman-leaders of the rebellion, anyway. And a hope leaped wildly into his thoughts, to see good old Brother Hari again, to try to, in some unknown way, make up for all the ills he had wrought and attempted on both Hari and Nephew Vaskos. First, he would . . .

"Well?" the High Lord prodded. "Can you accept my offer, Lord Drehkos? Or will you need to return to Vawnpolis to confer with your staff?"

By great force of will, Drehkos managed to stop the dizzy spinning of his brain and to frame a reply of sorts. "In many respects, my lord, your offer is most generous. But why must you persecute the priests and monks? I know of no one of them who ever has lifted steel against the established order, either here or in Morguhn."

Milo looked grim. "No, Lord Drehkos, they but set others to do their dirty work for them; consciously aiding and abetting the evil designs of their devilish *kooreeooe*, they worked upon the minds of their followers, inflamed them with fiery oratory, and cleverly administered drugs when the time was ripe, and set them on a course of murder and destruction which was completely against the best interests of those poor, deluded followers.

"No, Lord Drehkos, I'll not suffer such conscienceless, merciless cowards to roam at large in my domains. As for the Initiates, I . . . Tell me, what know you of their rites?"

Drehkos shrugged. "Very little, I fear, my lord. After all, had the rites not been kept secret, there would have been no Mysteries, would there?"

"Quite true," smiled the High Lord, then became once more serious of mien, deadly serious. "Know you then, Lord Drehkos, that these Mysteries were a debauched, depraved, hideously perverted distortion of true Christianity. In the foul rites of the Inner Mysteries, men and women were tortured and mutilated, innocent little children—babes, even—were hacked apart and the hot blood of their living, screaming bodies mixed with wine and other substances to be greedily guzzled by these same Initiates."

Captain Pehtros had paled visibly. Captain Djaimz looked greenish and ill; Drehkos sat, rigid, in his chair, his big hands clenched together so that the scarred knuckles shone white as new snow. He had, secretly, long suspected that some awful practices were part and parcel of the Inner Mysteries, but it had been simply a gut feeling with no real grounds for its existence. Nonetheless, he found the High Lord's words, terrible as they were, easy to believe.

"Such was the worst," Milo continued to his abashed audience, "but it was far from all. Sexual orgies frequently were the climax to their 'services,' and, since a child to sacrifice was not always available, they also filled their communion cup with animal blood, human urine and even women's moonblood."

Captain Djaimz's chair crashed over and the young officer stumbled hurriedly from the chamber, both hands pressed to his lips.

"But . . . but, my lord, why?" Drehkos shook his head in wonderment. "Such practices are no part of any religion I've ever heard of, and I've read of many, both modern and ancient."

Milo's wide shoulders rose and fell. "There are some similarities to the old Ehleen monster cults which flourished in the last few years before the coming of the Horseclans, a hundred and fifty years ago. But, beyond those, I can but surmise that the witchmen-*kooreeooee* extemporaneously concocted their ceremonies, since there were significant differences between those described by Spiros and those described by Mahreeos.

"As to why! Principally, because they are evil men to whom the sufferings and debasements of others mean absolutely nothing. In order to draw one foot closer to their goals, they would cheerfully bring about the deaths of half the population of the Confederation. And such is about what would have happened had their nefarious scheme come to full fruition."

Drehkos looked his puzzlement. "I . . . I don't understand . . ." he began, but Milo cut him off.

"Nor will you, *vahrohneeskos*, until yon city is once more in Confederation hands and I have your oaths of fealty. Officially, you're still a rebel, an enemy, and I'm too old a dog to willingly give you an edge."

The rebel commander drained off the last of his wine and stared for a long minute into the empty cup. At length, he set it on the table before him, rose from his chair, unhooked his cased sword from his baldric and laid it on the board, its worn hilt near the High Lord's hand. Following his lead, Captain Pehtros did the same. Captain Djaimz, his face and armor splashed with water, reentered just in time to add his own weapon to the formal surrender.

Chapter III

Vahk Vrainyuhn watched his runty mountain pony crop at the few spears of dead grass poking through the snow, and shivered, his teeth chattering. But it was neither the biting cold nor the bitter wind which had so set *Dehrehbeh* Vahk, a mountain warrior born and inured to cold, to trembling. No, it was the proximity to the sinister Valley of the Maidens.

Looking back to the fire, around which his score of warriors were quietly finishing their meal of venison and mush, Vahk could feel their fear, as well. Only their inborn loyalty to him, their hereditary *dehrehbeh*, had kept them camped three months in this place of waking-sleeping dread; just as only his own unquestioning obedience to the will of the great chief, the *nahkhahrah*, had sent him and them as escort to the Woman-of-Powers, who had entered the Pass of the Maidens moon-before-last, bidding them await her return.

Vahk and his warriors were not men easily frightened. Weak or craven Ahrmehnee children did not survive to adulthood, and these were picked fighters, the very cream of the Vrainyuhn tribe; not a one but had trophies racked in the House of Skulls. As for Vahk himself, he had, when a herdboy of less than one hundred seventy moons, slain a prowling bear-sow, first driving her off the goat she had slain, then receiving her ferocious charge on his spear; firm, he had held, heedless of the claws which savaged arms and shoulders and face, until the wide blade found and burst her fierce heart. Too, he had taken men's heads, many heads, his first when he was but something less than two hundred moons.

The Ahrmehnee tribes were much feared by all their neighbors, mountaineer and lowlander alike, and with good and sufficient cause. They had dwelt in the mountain valleys—and, formerly, in the foothills, as well—since the

28

World Death ended the Time of the Gods, were themselves the descendants of gods. The Ehleenee, strive as they might for near six thousand moons, had come away well bloodied, leaving behind many heads, on each occasion they had tried to lessen the constant menace of Ahrmehnee raids. Only a Confederation army of more than one hundred thousand men had finally driven them from their foothills, and then they had fled only because there were too few warriors left to effectively fight in open country.

Ten times thirteen moons later, the surviving elder warriors led the next generation of black-haired, hook-nosed young headhunters in an attempt to reclaim their stolen foothills; but they met their match for reckless courage and fierce bloodthirstiness in the hard-fighting horse archers of Clans Baikuh, Vawn and Skaht. Even so, they might have conquered through sheer weight of numbers, had not the Undying Devil of the Confederation returned and, with another huge army, crushed them at the Battle of Bloody Ford.

So few men had come back to the mountains after that defeat that nearly thirty times thirteen moons had elapsed ere the tribes had regained near to their former strength. And by then, the *stahn* was being severely pressed from both west and northwest by numerous, though primitive, non-Ahrmehnee peoples.

The Thirteen Tribes had stopped the newcomers, of course, but not decisively. The Muhkohee, as they were called after the name of one of their principal tribes, had settled on the fringes of Ahrmehnee lands, and the fight was now of many hundreds of moons duration, each new generation blooding itself on the ancient foe, race against race raiding race for goats and food in hard winters, for women and heads anytime. Quarter was neither asked nor given, the few warriors taken alive were invariably tortured to death . . . very, very slowly, sight and smell and sound of their agonies being always most pleasing to their captors.

Naturally, the Ahrmehnee still raided their former lands, bringing back fat cattle and sheep, fine, tall horses, choice, high-spirited women, heads and much rare booty. But these raids were small, hit-and-run affairs, and the *nahkhahrah* always forbade any tribe's raiders to penetrate far into the border duchies. For another decimation like Bloody Ford would, today, spell the certain extirpation of the entire Ahrmehnee *stahn* under the ravening spears and knives of the barbaric Muhkohee: nought but justified fear of the thousands of grim warriors the Thirteen Tribes could muster held their enemies in any sort of check.

No, Ahrmehnee warriors feared neither man nor beast . . . but they, one and all, feared the Maidens unashamedly . . . and no one of them could say why.

Vahk and his race knew very little about the Maidens, save that, like the Ahrmehnee themselves, they worshiped the Lady Moon, wore strange and antique-looking armor, were stark warriors and paid for such items as their delegations came to Ahrmehnee villages to buy in silver and gold coins of unusual uniformity which bore likenesses of men and women and beasts as well as legends which not even the wisest Ahrmehnee elders could decipher.

Their valley was very large, virtually inaccessible and well guarded, having but a single known entry. It was before the yawning, black mouth of this cavern that Vahk's tribesmen now were encamped. The mountains surrounding the Valley of the Maidens presented an almost uniform facade of weathered rock and deep, dusty runnels. Such terrain was difficult for goats or men, impossible for ponies, but even so, the crests of the high ridges connecting the mountains showed the viewer an unbroken stretch of rough-dressed stone walls, crenellated and set with towers, squatting amid the dark evergreens.

The old tales said that Maidens had been inhabiting the valley when the ancestors of the Thirteen Tribes first came to the hills and mountains. They, like the Ahrmehnee, were God-spawned. And these two sacred races had lived with peace between them for moons beyond reckoning.

But for all their similarities of worship, their shared glorious ancestry, their relatively friendly relations and the fact that the Ahrmehnee were renowned far and wide for their lustiness and those Maidens who ventured forth from their hold were right often young, comely and toothsome—albeit a mite on the muscular side with breasts invariably concealed beneath armor—there never had been intermarriage or even casual fraternization. In the course of the years, hot-headed or drunken Ahrmehnee had, on occasion, sought to seduce or force one of the Maidens; the would-be seducers had met with cold rebuff, the rapists with quick and bloody death.

It was supposed that men did dwell in that mysterious

Valley, for the Maidens were not Undying—they aged like all living creatures and, after a while, came no more to buy goods in the villages, their places being taken by other, younger Maidens. But no one could say for sure, since no one had ever seen a man of the Maidens' race, nor managed ever to even glimpse of what lay beyond dark entry cavern and wall-crowned summits. The *nahkhahrah* had always strictly forbidden Ahrmehnee to trespass up the bare, rocky slopes, and those few who had seen fit to disobey had never been seen again.

The scattering of villages near to the Valley sometimes witnessed weird and disturbing phenomena—sustained and awful rumblings from within the hold, accompanied by roiling layers of thick smoke by day and unearthly radiances by night; and, for many days after, the cataract which fell from those heights and the mountain river it fed would be oddly hued and fetid to both nose and taste. And the phenomena and mysteries had given rise to a plethora of terrible tales. Some were believed, some half-believed, most used only to frighten naughty children. But told and retold over the centuries, they had given rise to the fears and dreads which had made these last three moons so unpleasant for Vahk and his fighters. Like most Ahrmehnee, they normally avoided coming within a mile of the mouth of the cavern, for all that the approach was gently graded and wide enough for two horsemen abreast.

Nor, reflected Vahk, would they now be within forty miles of this place, had it not been for the comings of the People-of-Powers. The first snows were buried under their successors and the surplus cattle were being slaughtered for salting, when the two men and the woman rode into the village of the *nahkhahrah*, in company with old *Dehrehbeh* Hahgohn Kohehnyuhn, who was come with his party for the Council of the *Kehv* Moon.

In the Council House, lit by fat-lamps made from skulls, the pock-faced, white-haired Hahgohn, whose tribe occupied the southernmost of the lands held by Ahrmehnee, arose and told the *nahkhahrah* and the other eleven *dehrehbehee* of how the three strangers had been brought to him by a village headman, of how they all three spoke to him in fluent—if somewhat archaic—Hahyahs, and told of having been sent by Moon to aid Moon's faithful people in regaining their ancient lands.

"And my father, my brothers," the eldest of the

dehbehrehee had concluded, "I am convinced that they speak truly, for they surely are wondrous in their ways, commanding strange devices of thunder and lightning which can slay at two and three bowshots' distance and sharing ownership of a pair of chests—each no bigger than a common travel chest—which," he lowered his voice, "contain *living men!*"

Of course, no one had believed old Hahgohn's preposterous tales . . . not at first. But the *nahkhahrah* had been sufficiently titillated to first speak with the leader of the strangers, then with all three, and by the time he brought them to the Council House, he was as fervent as had been Kohehnyuhn, earlier.

Vahk paused in his musings to tuck his sodden cloak more tightly at the neck, shivering at the icy touch of the fabric on his bare throat. He shivered again, then, under his breath, promised a white buck-goat next moonbirth, if only Lady Moon would grant that the Woman-of-Powers rejoin them *today* . . . or even tomorrow.

Sahrah Sahrohyuhn (otherwise known as Erica Arenstein, D. Sc.) stepped onto the back of the kneeling man, and from that human mountingblock bestrode her fine riding mule—every bit as surefooted as the stunted mountain ponies of the Ahrmehnee, yet as big and powerful as the Maidens' warhorses.

Once in the saddle, Sahrah/Erica was more than anxious to be upon her way back to the cold, primitive village of the *nahkhahrah*. For all that her mission had been crowned with greater success than expected, for all that the Maidens and their rulers had made her more than welcome, she had not been comfortable since she first entered this valley. She knew, could recognize, what its inhabitants could not.

Though cruel winter clamped the surrounding mountains and valleys in its icy teeth, flowers bloomed and grain rippled on the valley floor. Snow or sleet turned liquid as soon as it touched the ground, so that the worst winter weather became only soft mists in the Valley of the Maidens. Only the Watchers, posted on the circuit of walls high above, ever tasted of the sufferings of those who dwelt in the surrounding lands, for Maidens never quitted their comfortable hold in winter. They accepted the bounties of their goddess, appeasing Her with bloody sacrifices on those frequent occasions when She vented Her anger in fire, choking smoke and shuddering, quaking earth.

But the training and experience of Dr. Erica Arenstein could identify this paradisical-seeming valley for what it truly was, though it would have been foolish—suicidal, even—to attempt to impart this knowledge to the Maidens. It gave Sahrah/Erica the willies to awaken in the morning and see a column of smoke spiraling up from the Sacred Crescent, and the ominous rumbling which often accompanied it made her want to scream and run as far and as fast as this body could. So she was overjoyed to be leaving.

However, her months of well-concealed terror had been worthwhile. Large as it was, the valley was already crowded, and for two generations the Maidens had been forced to buy grain and other foodstuffs in order to feed the burgeoning population. Not much persuasion had been necessary to convince the rulers that the Will of the Goddess lay behind this opportunity to fight in concert with the neighboring tribes and win more land—good land, rich nonmountainous land.

Then, too, there was the Maidens' treasure, which the Center could put to good use, once Erica and Greenberg and Dr. Diamond had perfected a scheme to get it to their advance base. But it was both bulky and heavy, and many, many pack ponies would be necessary to transport it through those hundreds of miles of mountains. And they'd need a strong force to seize and guard the tons of gold ingots and ancient coins; perhaps they could recruit from the Muhkohee tribes, once the Maidens, Ahrmehnee and Confederation forces were busily butchering each other.

At the head of the long column of mounted and armored warrior women, Sahrah/Erica rode knee to knee with the tall, handsome *brahbehrnuh* or warleader of the Maidens. And she thought it was too bad, in a way, that that splendid body would most likely be hacked into bloody gobbets before the spring came on the hills. It was a strong, healthy and attractive body, for which she would willingly have traded the one she now occupied.

Milo Morai had not, in something less than two centuries, built his Confederation by passively awaiting attacks. In this present world, pacifism was suicidal, if indeed, it had not always been. Which was why, immediately Vawnpolis was surrendered and regarrisoned, he set about preparing for an offensive thrust into the mountains.

They gathered within the largest chamber of the Vawnpolis Citadel—the major nobles of the archduchy, with surrogates taking the places of those *thoheeksee* dead or incapacitated; the *strahteegoee* of the Confederation units camped outside the walls, headed by Sir Ehdt, the siegemaster, and High Lady Aldora; *Vahroneeskos* Drehkos Daiviz of Morguhn and three of his officers, all veterans of his early-summer march through the mountains.

Working from such few maps as were available, Sir Ehdt had constructed a huge sand-table model of the western borders of Vawn, with southernmost Skaht to the north and northernmost Baikuh to the south. Now, he and a couple of Confederation officers were tracing Drehkos' route and altering the model to conform with the former rebels' memories of the terrain through which they had fought.

And, throughout it all, *Thoheeks* Bili of Morguhn had sat in his place, silently staring his hatred at the gray-haired, emaciated figure of his rebellious former vassal. Only some exceedingly firm language from Milo and Aldora had gotten the young noble into the same room with Drehkos, for Bili could not forget the siege of Morguhn Hall or that Drehkos had been one of the rebel commanders there. His pride might keep the fact from his clansmen, but his peers well knew that pardoning Drehkos and the mad *Vahrohnos* Myros had been a bitter pill for Bili to swallow.

Sir Ehdt's pointer paused over the serpentine line of light-blue sand which represented the principal nonseasonal waterway debouched by this section of mountains. When he spoke, his voice was tinged with the respect which the *vahrohneeskos* had earned from those who had fought him so long. "Lord baronet, this blue sand is the main stream of the Peekrohs River, which you must have crossed next. Please try to recall just where you crossed and the approximate depth." He then handed over the pointer.

Fingering his ear with his free hand, Drehkos briefly closed his eyes in concentration, then moved up to the table, scrutinizing the jagged chunks of rock and hummocks of sand. Beckoning his officers to him, he exchanged a few low-voiced words with them, then spoke aloud.

"As we remember, my lords, we entered Bitter River about here . . . but came out here." He indicated a spot some little distance downstream of the point of entry.

Before he could say more, *Vahrohnos* Rai Fraizehr, sitting as surrogate for the infant heir of dead *Thoheeks* Fraizehr, nodded. "Aye, those mountain streams be swift. How many men and horses did you lose in that crossing?"

But Drehkos shook his close-cropped head. "It was only swift in the center channel, my lord, though fortunately not too deep. For the length of the distance, here, it is very wide, but generally shallow. That's why we stayed in it for so long—it's a pebble bed and easier going for tired horses and exhausted or wounded men than the trails which paralleled it."

He frowned. "Besides which something *told* me to employ that route and—"

"And, my lords," put in one of the former rebel officers with a grin, "Lord Drehkos' hunch was right, as they mostly are. A couple of days after, we took a wounded Ahrmehnee and, ere he died, squeezed out of him the information that an ambush was set and waiting for us just where we would have been about an hour after we forded the river had we gone straight across. Thanks to Lord Drehkos, we outfoxed those barbarian bastards, went near two whole days without having to fight, we did!" crowed Captain Toorkos, exultantly.

Milo, Aldora and Sir Ehdt had already questioned Drehkos and almost every other living survivor of that march at great length. This session was being staged for the benefit of the nobles and army officers. Now the High Lord rose from his place.

"As you are aware, gentlemen, it is my intent to invade the Ahrmehnee mountains in force. It will be a savage and brutal campaign, for they must be hit hard and hurt seriously, else we'll soon have them here in our laps."

Striding around the table, he took up the pointer and placed its tip at the Gap of Vawn—where the transmontane trade-road entered the mountains and near to which lay the tumbled ruins of Fort Buhkuh, in which the last of the Vawnee Kindred nobility had resisted to their deaths the Vawnee rebels.

"At this gap will strike the main body of our force, led

by me. I will lead most of the Confederation infantry, with three squadrons of *kahtahfraktoee, Thoheeks* Hwahltuh of Vawn-Sanderz and his clansmen and half of *Vahrohneeskos* Drehkos' troops. We will strike directly for the heart—the seat of the *Stahn Nahkhahrah*, himself, the place called Zeese."

He moved the pointer northward, up into the duchy of *Thoheeks* Skaht. "The force which enters Raider Gap will be led by the High Lady. It will consist of eight squadrons of *kahtahfraktoee*, two of lancers, *Vahrohneeskos* Drehkos and all of his remaining cavalry and the Kindred nobility of Skaht, Duhnkin, Lahmahnt and Fraizehr."

Rapidly, he moved the pointer south, into the Duchy of Baikuh. "Through the Gap of Skulls will go the third prong of our attack. All the Freefighters presently with the army, all the Kindred nobility not otherwise assigned, all to be led by *Thoheeks* Bili of Morguhn."

Months agone, when Bili had been the youngest and newest duke of the archduchy and an unknown quantity to his peers, there would certainly have been loud and bitter outcry at the High Lord's choice of commanders for the southernmost column. But in the wake of several months of brutal combat, much of it commanded by Bili, he was no longer the newest *thoheeks* and his abilities as both astute captain and stark warrior were well known and unquestioned . . . for all his not-quite-nineteen years.

The High Lord continued: "The prairiecats will be evenly divided amongst the three columns, as will the medical personnel. The engineers and selected Confederation Army units will take up garrison duties in Vawnpolis and the border forts. The trains will remain in Vawnpolis, as well, but in readiness, for there may be need of them. Overall command of the defenses of the three duchies will be in the capable hands of Sir Ehdt Gahthwahlt and, after due consideration, I have decided that *Sub-strahteegos* Vaskos Daiviz of Morguhn will command Vawnpolis, assisted by former *keeleeoostos Vahrohneeskos* Ahndros Theftehros of Morguhn."

Of all nonmutants present, only Bili understood the hidden meaning of the High Lord's choices—Aldora was a farspeaker, whose mind could range the Vawnpolis base or any of the other two columns at will; using the added power of another mind, preferably that of a prairiecat, Milo, Bili or Ahndros could do the same, and so the farflung commands would be in frequent or constant contact, as the situations demanded.

One of the *strahteegoee*—a short, chunky, white-haired man, whose helm-creased brow and silver cat pendant served notice that he was a field officer, not an administrator—stood, cleared his throat and said, "My lord Milo . . . ?"

Milo smiled. "Senior *Strahteegos* Paidros Kailehb has a question, as usual."

Everyone laughed or chuckled; it was a standing joke. Even Bili's scowl softened into a smile.

Unabashed, the officer went on. "My lord, if we are to leave the trains behind, how are our necessary supplies to be transported? Mules? If so, we had best commence gathering them."

The High Lord nodded. "A herd of five hundred mules and asses should, even now, be moving down through Skaht and will be here in a few days. Only my column will bear any quantity of supplies, however, The High Lady's cavalry and *Thoheeks* Bili's Freefighters will be expected to subsist on game—and the mountains are, we understand, swarming with wild beasts—and what foodstuffs they seize from the Ahrmehnee.

"But, back to the order of march and the responsibilities of the three columns, gentlemen. If the Witchmen are physically present among the Ahrmehnee the logical place for them to be is with the *nahkhahrah*. This is why my column will strike directly for his village. Only one tribe, aside from the *nahkhahrah's* own, lies athwart our route, the Tribe of Frainyuhn—or its southern fringes. I anticipate little danger from them, however, since I met their chief last year and found him a young hothead, such a one as tends to make a poor defensive warrier."

Under his shaven scalp, Bili's brow wrinkled. "But, my lord, if the Witchmen are with the *nahkhahrah*, will not most or all of the warriors of the Thirteen Tribes be there as well?"

"Just so," grinned the High Lord. "And this is where Aldora's work and yours begins. The plan of the Witchmen is to neutralize—by hook or by crook—the non-Ahrmehnee tribes to the north and west so that the Ahrmehnee fighters will not need to leave warriors to protect their valleys and mountain villages. For though they bear allegiance to the *nahkhahrah*, Ahrmehnee family ties are far stronger, and they will desert the *nahkhahrah* in an eyeblink if their homes are imperiled.

"Now, the lands of eight of the tribes are situated to the south of the *nahkhahrah's* seat. From one end of this coast to the other, Freefighters are justly renowned as reavers and rapers. And they are to have free rein, Bili. I want every village leveled, every flock butchered or dispersed. Kill the men and rape the women and run the survivors into the forests. But make certain that there *are* survivors and that they *do* get away—headed north, preferably on ponyback. When the lands of the first tribe are laid waste, move quickly on to the next.

"The High Lady's column will also be performing atrocities upon the three tribe lands which lie north of the *nahkhahrah's* holdings, and by the time my column arrives at its objective, I expect that most of the Ahrmehnee warriors will be widely scattered, battling back to their homes . . . or what will then be left of them. We should then be able to coerce the Ahrmehnee into handing over the damned Witchmen, as well as hostages for their future good behavior. Then we can move the Regulars north and south to help in scotching the rest of the Witchmen's schemes."

Chapter IV

Halfway up the last, steep slope, Pehroosz Bahrohnyuhn first heard the terrified bleating of the goats and the snorting-stamping of horses or ponies. Hill-born and bred, for all that her father was village headman and full brother to Chief Moorahd, the proud-breasted, raven-haired girl was immediately suspicious. Dropping the bundle of fresh-baked bread she had been bringing to her younger brothers, she forsook the narrow track for the bordering thick growth of evergreens and gingerly crept upward seeking a point from which she might see the whole of the pasture slopes without being seen herself.

It was a scene of horror. Big men on big, lowland horses were cantering about the pasture slopes, sabering or axing the scuttling, bleating goats. The dry winter grass already was speckled with quivering, bloody carcasses. Of her two youngest brothers there was no sign, but Toorkohm—at a hundred and forty-three moons, thirty-seven moons her junior; big-boned, with their father's craggy face, wide shoulders and quick, sure movements—stood at bay, his back to the dry-stone chimney of the herdsmen's shelter, his wolfspear held menacingly ready, fresh blood glowing on its wide blade.

Pehroosz could not repress a smile of grim satisfaction, even under these conditions, for one scale-shirted raider lay stretched on the sward, his throat gaping like a huge second mouth, his chest and shoulders covered with frothy pink gore. Another sat swaying with agony, while a third labored to stop his life from leaking out the broad stab in his thigh. It was obvious that Toorkohm had fought skillfully and well.

But it could not last, this Pehroosz knew. No matter how reckless his courage, how strong his arm, how thirsty his spear, he was but a largish, unarmored boy, now ringed by cautiously advancing, fully armed, full-grown raiders. It ended quickly. A long-bladed saber licked out and Toorkohm sought to parry it with his spearshaft. With a practiced drawcut, the raider's upper edge sliced deeply into the seasoned walnut wood. In the moment the spear was immobilized, two more raiders stepped close to Pehroosz's brother and she quickly closed her eyes as the blades rose and fell, rose and fell with the meaty *tchunnks* reminiscent of autumn hog-butchering. Toorkohm's own, thin death wail rose above those of the goats he had fought so well to succor.

Her pretty olive face bathed with tears, Pehroosz slowly worked her broad-hipped but lissome body back from the crest, not turning until the bulk of the hill loomed above her. And what she saw then brought a piercing scream from her throat. Then consciousness left her.

The chill awakened her, and she instinctively sought to flex her body against it, but neither arms nor legs would move. Only when she opened her eyes could she see that she was lying on the packed-earth floor of the herdsmen's hut, her clothing all stripped from her and wadded beneath her buttocks. One of the raiders knelt his weight on her palms, holding her arms extended above her head; two others crouched grinning, their big, dirty hands locked about her ankles, splaying her long legs. Standing between those legs was a fourth raider. His breeks were tumbled about his boot tops and he was tucking up the skirt of his scaleshirt. Pehroosz's first thought had been to show the bravery of her dead brother, but when she saw the thick, throbbing maleness standing up from the raider's loins, terror sent a shudder coursing through her body and a whimper bubbling from her lips.

She was deflowered savagely, brutally. And when the spent raider rose from her ravaged flesh, his place was taken by another. Then, another . . . and another . . . and yet another.

Pehroosz lost count of the number of attacks. But at some point she did rally, did do something other than scream her throat raw. She tried to clench her pain-racked body and, failing that, bit at her tormentors, drawing blood from at least one, possibly two. But their buffets dizzied her and they began to hold themselves up and away from those teeth while they used her.

Somewhere close by, Pehroosz could hear the ugly, guttural sounds of some animal's agony. The noises were

harsh, sickening, and she wished that the raiders would saber the poor beast so that the noises would stop. Dimly,
from far off, she heard, too, men speaking in one of the
Mehruhkuhn dialects, but she had never had cause to master Mehrikan, since Ahrmehnee men did all the trading.

"I know just what Duke Bili ordered," snapped the
plate-armored officer shortly, the knuckles of his bridle
hand glowing white where he gripped the pommel of his
fine broadsword. "But if, Sword forbid, her screams carried as far north as they did south the whole damned village could be alerted by now! You, Grohz, put up your
damned dirk! Remember, we *want* the likes of this poor
girl to escape north to the *nahkhahrah*. All you men get
mounted now, put Patuhzuhn's body on his horse and
form up. Komees Hari will soon be at the ford, and we're
to meet him there. He wants to be in position to attack the
village just at the nooning. Run off the smaller ponies, but
leave the big one for her."

With a chuckle, the sergeant commented, "Sir Geros,
that chit were a maid, ere my yard rendered her a woman.
With the swiving we done give her, her crotch'll be sorer
nor a boil for some little while. She'll not be forking no
pony this day, I trow!"

His laughter was echoed by most of the others as they
strode out to the horses.

Shortly, a jingling and creaking and measured hoofbeats
receded into the distance as the patrol went back the way
they had come. But it was more than an hour before
Pehroosz, once more shivering in her nakedness, managed
to drag her bruised, battered body to the hearth, on which
a small fire still glowed.

She wished that the raiders had had the decency to slay
that still-suffering goat, ere they left. Some time later, she
realized that those hurt-animal sounds came not from a
goat, but from her own throat. Her fierce. Bahrohnyuhn
pride had refused to show the raiders her tears, but now
they came. In a great racking rush they came, and her
abused body doubled upon itself and shook to her sobs of
rage and pain and shame.

In his youth, *Komees* Hari Daiviz of Morguhn had been
a Freefighter, soldiering the length and breadth of the
Middle Kingdoms, whose two-score-plus principalities had
seen precious few years of peace in the four centuries

since the Great Earthquake had brought them into squab-
bling existence. The passage of more than a score of years
had failed to dim his memories of those bloody days, nor
had the pursuits of peace—marriage and the rearing of a
family, succession to his patrimonial title and estate, the
ordering of his lands and horses and people—softened him
or expunged from his mind the hard lessons learned from
the particularly savage and merciless brand of warfare
peculiar to the kingdoms of the north.

Almost all of the Freefighters who had ridden into the
mountains behind *komees*' suzerain, *Thoheeks* Bili
Morguhn of Morguhn, were men born and bred and
blooded in the Middle Kingdoms, and Hari had quickly
reverted to the man he had been twenty-odd years before,
finding that he once more was thinking like a professional
soldier. He was again relishing the rough banter and lewd
songs; the constant and often senseless profanities and
blasphemies fell unnoticed on his ears and unconsciously
from his lips. It seemed the most natural thing in the
world to end a hard day's march with a bruising session of
sword-fencing or staffplay, under the discriminating eye of
a weaponsmaster—which breed of noncom tyrannically
chivvied exhausted officers and men alike into nightly
practice sessions in weapons skills.

In recognition of his experience, the *thoheeks* had given
him command of a squadron of dragoons and had not de-
murred too vociferously when the old *komees* chose one of
the suzerain's favorites, the valorous Sir Geros
Lahvoheetos of Morguhn, to be his senior captain.

At their last meeting, the young *thoheeks* had stood before Hari and the other squadron commanders in his
three-quarter armor, with a cold wind whipping his oiled
cloak about his booted legs and the rays of new-risen
Sacred Sun glinting on the brass point atop the shaft of
the Red Eagle banner, ensign of the House of Morguhn.

The scarred, deeply tanned face which peered from the
opened helm gave no indication of the tall, broad-shoul-
dered nobleman's actual youth. The high forehead was
furrowed and a web of tiny wrinkles crinkled the outer
corners of the blue-gray eyes. His baritone voice flat and
emotionless, he reiterated the High Lord's orders and instructions with regard to their mission and its implementa-
tion. Then he drew his broadsword and used it to point

out features of the parchment map which a couple of men held unrolled behind him.

"Gentlemen, Sir Ehdt emphasizes that he cannot claim more than a bare minimum of accuracy for this map. Unlike the northern and central columns, ours will not be traversing lands scouted out by Drehkos-the-traitor last year. The only references Sir Ehdt had were campaign sketches and notes at least three generations old, plus the questionable information of some traveling merchants. Nonetheless, it is all we have, and so we must make do with it.

"We are now here, at this crossroads. The column will march west today, dropping off squadrons as it goes. When your squadron leaves the column, you are on your own, gentlemen, on your own. There is little likelihood that you will encounter more than a bare sprinkling of Ahrmehnee warriors, since most of the bastards are up there in the north; but don't forget, these are their mountains. They know every nook, crag and cranny and they are past masters of irregular warfare, so even two or three will cost you heavily if you let them take you unaware.

"If the terrain will permit, do not allow your troopers to ride bunched up, where a volley or a boulder could do real damage, for we'll be covering a forty-mile front and we want at least a peek into every valley and vale. It would not only be disobedient to our orders to leave a single village untouched, but very dangerous, as well, since we need our enemy fleeing before us, not skulking behind.

"You are all seasoned campaigners, else I'd not have placed you in command positions, so I'll not insult your intelligence by lecturing you on dos and don'ts and the merits of basic preparedness. After all," he treated them to a fleeting grin, "you're commanding Freefighters who can forage for necessities, if need be, and don't require the careful spoonfeeding of Confederation Regulars."

Hari had joined in the brief chortling and chuckling. If the siege of Vawnpolis had taught them nothing else, they had all learned the essential superiority of the Freefighter and the Kindred nobility to the vaunted and highly trained Army of the Confederation.

At first, the strict discipline and unquestioning obedience to orders, the machinelike precision of movements and maneuvers, of the serried ranks of Regulars had impressed them. But that was before they had seen the other side of the coin. The discipline was exacted at the cost of the men's individuality; the obedience robbed them of any initiative, and the precision had conditioned them into virtually will-less robots. The spectacle of a regiment's even, ordered ranks trotting inexorably against an enemy position, emotionlessly dressing to fill the gaps left by killed or wounded comrades, halting as one man on order to hurl close-range volleys of darts, then raising a guttural cheer and pouring over their objective, was awe-inspiring. But the helplessness of the men of the same regiment in any case not covered by rules and regulations, when no officer or noncom was about to think for them, sickened and repelled the self-reliant condottieri and most of the freedom-worshiping noblemen, even as the habit of most Confederation officers of treating anyone not of equal or higher military rank as a bull-headed child irked and infuriated them.

"I'll dole out the flesh tailors as far as they'll go," the *thoheeks* went on. "But there're just not enough of them, and anyone wounded in a squadron lacking them will just have to take his chances with a good horseleech.

"Each squadron will be allowed twelve mules, no more. And any officer I catch wasting a muleback to pack a tent will get my boot up his arse; this be no pleasure jaunt and, if it's shelter you must have, take it from the Ahrmehnee."

His swordtip traced a course north from the trade road. "Mark you this route on your small maps, gentlemen. When the last of your squadrons is on the way, I'll set out on this path behind you with the five reserve squadrons and the remainder of the packtrain. When, eventually, you encounter sizable numbers of Ahrmehnee warriors, send gallopers back for me, then choose a tenable position and hold it until I arrive. *On no account* is any squadron to attempt either to push through or to retreat before the main Ahrmehnee host! Understood?"

Sheathing his broadsword and signing his men to roll up the map, he smiled wolfishly. "Dispose of loot as you see fit, catch-as-catch-can or equal division, it's all to be yours, since the High Lord will claim no share, nor will I. Reave and rape and ravage to your hearts' content, put the fear of Sword into these barbarians. And don't stick at slaying children, either; nits make lice, and we want to so depopulate these mountains that the bastards will be at least another generation recovering.

"I'll probably have a few words with each of you, ere your squadron separates from the column. But for now, let's to horse. Good hunting, gentlemen."

That had been three days ago. Now Hari's main body was trotting up a long, narrow, twisting vale, towering dark-green mountains on their right and a swift-flowing rivulet on their left. Between broad patches of snow and dark, weathered outcrops of rock, the ground was crunchy with the stubble of sere, yellowed grass. Only goats or sheep would have cropped it so close.

Up ahead, nestled in a larger, more sheltered valley, lay the village his scouts had found yesterday. They had reported the only adult males to be either old or crippled, so Hari had elected to proceed at a normal march rate, though as quietly as possible so that the quarry might not be spooked and go to ground, and attack whenever he arrived in position. But since the scouts had also reported a number of flocks of goats scattered about the routes to the village, he had sent several squads on ahead to make certain that the herdsmen carried no warning to the objective.

All had seemed well and they had been rapidly advancing when that damned screaming had echoed down the vale, bouncing off the steep slopes on either hand. The screams had gone on and on and on, and, cursing the carelessness of whoever was responsible, while hoping that the intervening hills would keep this alarm from reaching ears in the village, Hari had sent young Sir Geros and a squad up to try to still the noise at its source.

As they came to where two smaller streams joined to form the larger, the knight rejoined *Komees* Hari, while the two squads trotted back to take places in the column.

"What in Sword was going on?" demanded the old nobleman immediately. "What occasioned those fornicating screams?"

"Just that, my lord, fornication . . . rather, a gang rape," Sir Geros replied grimly. "The squad had caught a girl on the trail leading from the village. She must have been a really beautiful girl, too, for she was still pretty even after all they'd done to her."

"Did they slay her?" inquired the komees idly.

"They would've, my lord, but I forbade such and, recalling what you said of the orders of the High Lord and Duke Bili, I had them leave a pony nearby for her. I should imagine that the tale of a raped wife or daughter would be most effective in persuading men to come back and defend their homes."

Hari chewed at his lower lip. "True enough, man, true enough. But it might be better to send a man back up there to cut her throat. What if she alerts the damned village?"

Geros shook his head to the extent his tight-laced helm would allow. "No need, my lord. She was taken by all twelve of the men, I think, and the sergeant as well. They used her badly, very badly. I doubt me she can even walk, much less mount a pony."

Hari shrugged. "Well, if you say so, lad. And besides, if we can keep up this pace, we'll probably be on the village ere she could get there, anyhow."

For long and long after no more tears would come, Pehroosz lay huddled near the fire, shuddering and sobbing dry sobs. But as the untended fire began to die, the shudders metamorphosed into shivers and the sobs into gasps between chattering teeth. Once, through the hard-packed dirt beneath her, she thought to feel the drumming of many hooves. Sure that the dread sounds heralded the return of her attackers, she huddled her aching body more tightly and whimperingly awaited the unendurable.

When a hairy something touched her and she felt hot, damp breath on her quivering flesh, she tried to scream, but her tight, strained throat emitted only a dull croaking sound. Gathering her courage, she opened her eyes to see what fresh horrors were to be her lot.

Above Pehroosz stood old Zahndrah, most venerable of the Bahrohnyuhn she-goats, her gentle, brown eyes pain-filled, mutely questioning the brutality which had been so unjustly dealt her. All along the nanny's right flank, the hair was crusty and brownish, marking the path of a shallow saber cut.

Raising a shaking hand, Pehroosz caressed the small, neat head between nose and cursive horns. Uttering soft sounds of pleasure, Zahndrah pressed closer, gently nuzzling the familiar-smelling human. Then she turned tail and knelt to display her milk-heavy udders.

Until then, Pehroosz had not realized just how thirsty she was. She looked about her, spotted a small, wooden bowl within easy reach. Reaching for the vessel, she sat up . . . then abruptly rolled back onto her hip, breathless with pain. After some experimenting, she found a relatively painless position and first filled, then drained off three bowls of hot, frothy milk. Relieved, Zahndrah arose and ambled back out of the shelter.

With the nanny's departure, Pehroosz began once more to suffer from the cold, so, careful not to let the most abused parts of her body come in contact with the hard, bumpy floor, she levered herself erect. But she could not remain so. Groaning at the sharp agony of the cramps racking her belly, she fell to her knees and elbows and so remained until, after eternities, the spasms subsided.

On hands and knees, she retraced the few feet to the scene of her defilement and, fighting to hold down the goatmilk, set her bruised and clumsy hands to unfolding the damp, sticky bundle of her clothing. But, since they had apparently been ripped from her by main force, homespun gown and shift and woolen overshift were only so much shredded cloth now. Only her cloak was whole. Gratefully, Pehroosz wrapped herself in the stained garment. She at first thought the cursed raiders must have stolen her fine fur-lined felt boots, but she found them, finally, tossed into a dark corner.

Before the small fire died away, she fed it bits and pieces of the stools which had been the shelter's only furnishings. Then, as a cold wind had commenced to angle in, she crawled to the open side and painfully worked the oiled hides down into place, eventually forcing her stiff fingers to properly lace them together and secure their bottoms. By the time she had finished, she was exhausted, and, lulled by this exhaustion, as well as by the warm near-darkness and the physical and emotional stress of the last few hours, she lapsed into a deep sleep, a healing sleep, from which she wakened only enough to feed such fuel as she had to the fire from time to time as needed.

The High Lord and his host camped below the Gap of Vawn, amid the tumbled, ghost-haunted ruins of Fort Buhkuh, until Bili's and Aldora's farspeak told him that the keen steel and fiery torches of their far-ranging forces were hard at their bloody task. Then, of a bitter, snowy morn, drums rolled, trumpets brayed and disciplined ranks of Confederation infantry set bootsole to trade road in the wake of the mounted vanguards and scouts. Each of the four regiments had been brought to full strength by the

addition of able-bodied former rebels from the Vawnpolis
garrison, and those officer-grade types not riding with
Vahrohneeskos Drehkos trotted their mounts along as su-
pernumeraries with the High Lord's staff. Only the sick or
disabled rebels had been left in Vawnpolis; plus, of course,
the lunatic *Vahrohnos* Myros Deskati of Morguhn, and his
"bodyguards" commanded by the faithful Captain Danos.

Two days' march into the mountains, the vanguard
squadron of *kahtahfrahktoee*—heavy cavalry—under command of *Keeleeohstos* Gaib Lihnstahk fought an inconclusive action with an unknown, but certainly small, number
of Ahrmehnee tribesmen. Had the ambush succeeded, vanguard casualties would surely have been heavy. But the
concealed bushwackers had been spied out by the swift,
fleeting prairiecats, who had reported the location to Gaib,
then lain in position to take the Ahrmehnee in flank and
rear at a critical point in the engagement. Certain articles
found on the bodies of the slain marked them as men of
the Ahrahkyuhn Tribe.

The following week saw four additional attempts of a
similar nature, all foiled by the keen senses of the mindspeaking felines who ranged point and flanks and rear of
the upward-toiling column. As the Ahrmehnee were
crafty, brave and on well-known home ground, their losses
were not truly heavy. Nonetheless, with the failure of the
fifth ambush, they ceased their attacks and the cats could
report no more than a handful, apparently pacing the
column.

They had been on the march for a fortnight when they
came to the charred ruins of the trade-road bridge jutting
blackly over the rushing waters of a tributary of the
Peekrohs River. Milo cursed himself for not foreseeing
such a likelihood and bringing at least a company or two
of the engineers. But cross the stream the army did, and
safely. Then a few hours' ascent brought them onto the
plateau which lay between the mountains of Tribe
Ahrahkyuhn—which they had just traversed—and those
inhabited by the tribe of the *nahkhahrah*, Tribe
Taishyuhn.

Amid the ancient, partially buried relics of a godcity,
the High Lord had a night camp erected. But on the mor-
row the march was not continued. Instead the men and
pack mules were put to the tasks of dragging timbers from
the slopes above and below, then raising a strong palisade

atop the usual earth mound. Some were even put to digging stones from their ages-old resting places and manhandling them into such positions as would give added strength to the defenses. The ground, hard and flinty under the best of conditions, was frozen and the work strenuous, but by the morning of the fourth day, Senior *Strahteegos* Hahfos could report the task completed.

Hahfos was young for a corps commander, barely forty summers, but such had been the attrition of officers—both senior and junior, company, field and *strahteegos* grades—at the savage siege of Vawnpolis, that the Morguhn Expeditionary Force was become an army composed principally of the young, the nimble and the lucky. Third son of a *thoheeks* whose lands lay far to the south and west near the shores of the vast inland sea, Hahfos Djohnz's appearance always pleased the High Lord, personifying as he did the splendid melding of two fine races—Horsclansman and Ehleen.

Two dozen years of campaigning had weathered his skin to the shade of old walnut and crosshatched all its visible surfaces with the seamed and puckered cicatrices which were the badge of his calling, but the High Lord accepted these scars and the permanent tan, unimpressed. Not yet bent by age, Hahfos stood one meter and three quarters; his close-cropped hair was almost the same shade as his face, with flashes of white at the temples, and though his blue-green eyes could chill an object of his displeasure to the innermost core, most occasions found them filled with merriment and joy of life.

A born leader of men, he had no need to rant and bellow, his orders were never pitched louder than the circumstances necessitated and he spoke either Mehrikan or Ehleeneekos tinged with the soft, slurring speech patterns of his faraway home. Astute as strategist and accomplished as tactician, he could be ferocious in personal combat, as was attested by the two Silver Cats he held; yet, withal, he was a kindly man and took no joy in needless suffering.

In the Fourteenth Regiment, which he had commanded for six years prior to his quite recent promotion, he had been affectionately known as "Old Pussyfoot." He had cared for his men and their response had been to give him not only an unflagging source of pride but their fierce love, as well. Not a few grizzled fighting men had openly wept when he left them for corps command.

When he had delivered his report to the High Lord, Milo nodded his thanks, then waved at the vacant chair across from his own. "If you've not something pressing, Hahfos, sit you down and have some of this abominable wine."

Hahfos' ready smile lit his face. "Thank you, mah lord."

Milo waited until the officer was seated and had poured and tasted the wine, then asked, "How heavy is your new mantle, good Hahfos? Do you wish you still were simply *sub-strahteegos* of the Fourteenth?"

Hahfos absently rubbed a horny forefinger up and down his short, slightly canted nose. "Yes, mah lord, sometimes. But then, when ah had the Fourteenth, ah sometimes wished ah still was simply a *keeleeohstos*, too. Ah suppose that all men think back on the days when things were comparatively easy, whenevah we're faced with difficulties we didn't have then."

"How true, how true," Milo sighed. "I sometimes think back to the freedom I enjoyed as a Horseclans chief, centuries ago. But tell me, how are you getting along with the regimental commanders? My staff informs me there's been a bit of friction since this march commenced."

"Only one real bone of contention exists, mah lord. Ah forbade certain gentlemen, whose ideas of discipline are somewhat at variance to mah own, from administering any moah than five lashes to any soldier within a given week. Ah pointed out that, since a man with twenty or thirty stripes can't mahch in ahmah and as we have no ambulances to carry them, they would weaken owah force were they to abide by their accustomed ways. Ah also pointed out that I had only two men flogged in six years, with no noticeable loss of discipline in the Fourteenth."

Milo grinned. "Good for you, Hahfos. Rubbed their noses in your successes, did you? I'd imagine that that galled them more than your order."

Hahfos shook his head. "Ah did not say what ah said to offend them, mah lord. But all ah said is true, mah lord! Ah *know*, ah *proved* mah views! The whip makes good men bad and bad men worse and it is, in any case, completely unnecessary. Advocates of the whip call it the 'Foundation of Discipline,' but it is no such thing, mah lord. If a commander be able and lets his men know that he cares for their welfare, he can easily maintain all the discipline needed with only rare application of the whip. Ah consider the whip to be the final argument of lazy or incompetent officers!"

He had waxed very vehement, now his tone softened. "Ah am sorry if ah offended mah lord, but mah lord did ask. . . ."

"No, Hahfos," Milo reassured him. "I was not offended. I could not agree more with most of it. But the cult of the whipping frame is hard to root out. It's a carryover custom from two centuries ago, from the pre-Horseclans Ehleen army, in which common spearmen were all peasants—to all intents and purpose, brutish and brutalized military slaves. I inherited that army intact and thought it best, at the time, to allow the Ehleenee officers to maintain most of their accustomed practices. When in later years I attempted to inaugurate new customs, I discovered the past ones to be so firmly entrenched from top to bottom that I would've chanced precipitating a virtual mutiny to force my will.

"But I was steeling myself to take that very chance, Hahfos. Then came the Second Kuhmbuhluhn War and, on its heels, the invasion by King Zenos VIII, and, since, we've seldom been at peace for any length of time."

"Ah understand, mah lord," said Hahfos sympathetically. "It is truly said that crowns and coronets can fast weigh down the spirit.

"But mah lord, ah . . . that is, would mah lord object if *ah* were to . . ."

Milo smiled once more. "Hahfos, you have free rein, my earnest prayers and all my approval. If you can do what you did with the Fourteenth with this corps, you will succeed old Ehmeekos as lord *strahteegos* of the armies, you have my solemn word on it."

Chapter V

Glumly, the *nahkhahrah* watched the last of the Gahrbehdyuhn Tribe depart his village, the ponies at a stiff trot, headed due south. As his assembled host had melted away, even as the accursed Undying Devil and his army had pressed farther and farther into the mountains, the temper of this chief of chiefs had worsened to the point where few men were now reckless enough to stray within easy reach of his fist or his ready raider's knife, especially when delivering bad news—and there was little news, these days, which was not bad.

The *nahkhahrah* could cheerfully have strangled each and every man of the departing tribe, but he immediately ruffled when a voice from close behind him said mockingly, "Soon my Maidens will be the only warriors in this dungheap village of yours, my valiant ally. This is the third tribe which has lost its courage and turned tail since the Undying Devil entered the mountains, is it not? Two tribes fled north and this one goes south. Where is the over-vaunted valor if its fierce Ahrmehnee? Or is that valor as much myth as are the tales you use to keep your womenfolk in bondage? Eh?"

Bristling, the *nahkhahrah* spun about to face his tormentor, knobby hand gripping the hilt of his big, heavy knife, worn, yellow teeth bared in a snarl of rage.

The *brahbehrnuh* did not twitch a muscle at his obvious threat. Though the two Maidens behind her tensed and fingered their hilts, she stood with her trousered legs spread wide, her arms akimbo. One of her attendants carried the *brahbehrnuh's* gold-plated helm, and the tall woman's glossy, black hair fell untrammeled, framing a strikingly handsome face. The full lips showed the even, white teeth in a mocking sneer, while the woman's ebon eyes glittered forth contempt.

There were no Ahrmehnee warriors anywhere close by,

52

and the *nahkhahrah*, though unquestionably brave, was not reckless. Grudgingly, he released his knife, growling. "Now, by Our Lady's Cusps, woman, I would Her emissaries had left you and your arrogant, unnatural breed in your hold! Had I mine own way—"

"But you do not!" snapped the *brahbehrnuh*, coldly. "Her dread Curse lies upon her or him who first breaks our alliance. Were it not so, I and mine would long since be back where we belong. Aye, and those of your poor, downtrodden women we could free with us!"

Pale and speechless with rage, the *nahkhahrah* brusquely pushed past the *brahbehrnuh* and her guards, limped into the council house and loudly slammed the thick door behind him, shooting the bolt for good measure. Stumping to his place, he simply sat, cracking his big knuckles, his scarred face working. And seeing the bloodlust shining from his eyes, no one of the nine *dehrehbehee* remaining asked any questions of him.

From the moment of entry into the village of the *brahbehrnuh* and her hundreds of armed, armored and supercilious female warriors, there had been tension of one sort or another. Obviously, the People-of-Powers had expected the tension to lessen and so had all felt free to leave on their mission to the Muhkohee tribes, but it had worsened, if anything. For one thing, burgeoning familiarity with the Maidens had virtually dissolved the semi-superstitious awe of them which many Ahrmehnee had had; for another, the blatant attempts of many of the Maidens to foment trouble between the *nahkhahrah's* tribesmen and their womenfolk or to seduce nubile maids and matrons into perverted sexual practices—which practices seemed to be endemic amongst the strutting, man-despising Maidens—had set all the Ahrmehnee warriors' teeth on edge and had caused the *nahkhahrah* ceaseless difficulties in preventing outright massacre of the vastly outnumbered "allies."

Early on, he had attempted to reason with the *brahbehrnuh*, had tried to persuade her to draw rein on her crudely antagonistic following, pointing out that unless she did so the only certain result would be the spilling of blood and that, considering the fact that she and hers were hundreds amidst thousands, a serious session in arms between Ahrmehnee and Maidens could end in but one way. It had been wasted breath and effort. The sow had heard him out, then insulted him, all the *dehrehbehee* and their Sacred Ancestors, obscenely; further, she had offered disparaging comments on all Ahrmehnee warriors, then on men in general. Then she had stalked from the council house, a mocking laugh floating behind her.

And the foul situation had worsened and worsened to the point at which the Council had had to actually execute three tribesmen who had drawn steel, in order to show the host that they were serious about maintaining the now shaky alliance. The *nahkhahrah* had taken to praying earnestly each night at moonrise that the People-of-Powers would soon return so that the projected invasion could get under way while he still could exercise a measure of control over his men.

Then, piling one mountain atop another, had come word that a great army, led by the Undying Devil called Meelohsh, was marching up the trade road, through the lands of the Frainyuhns, and he had bidden *Dehrehbeh* Hyk Frainyuhn and his tribesmen goodspeed and even reinforced them . . . with the worst of the troublemakers camped about.

But no plan or scheme of the unlucky young *dehrehbeh* had gone aright. Five times had he and his warriors set out to ambush the van of the invaders, five times had they been discovered, attacked and driven off with losses. The fifth failure had cost the life of Hyk himself, and the Frainyuhns had, predictably, withdrawn to their principal village to choose a new *dehrehbeh*, since the deceased had no living brothers old enough to lead.

So the *nahkhahrah* had sent out men to watch over the now unobstructed progress of the invading army, bidding them to keep much distance from the lowlanders, to flee if attacked and fight only if cornered. His orders had not been taken well by the Ahrmehnee, but out of respect for him they had voiced their disagreements out of his hearing.

Not so the Maidens, however. The insolent chits took to laughing at the old man whenever he rode at large, scornfully mocking his every word or gesture, frequently instigated and often led by the haughty *brahbehrnuh*.

But the *nahkhahrah* had suffered the criticism in silence, for he knew that his way was the right one. He was a very old man, far older than his appearance suggested. He had been chosen *nahkhahrah* when his aged father was slain fighting the lowlanders who had driven the Thirteen Tribes from the foothills and, a hundred and thirty moons later, he had led the Great Raid which had ended so disastrously at Bloody Ford.

He knew the fierce bravery of Ahrmehnee warriors and, much as he now hated the Maidens, he suspected that they might possibly be equally fine fighters. But his eyes had beheld thousands of valiant, stubborn Ahrmehnee cut down like ripe grain by the hosts of the Undying Devil. He knew that this present army slightly outnumbered his available forces. He knew that even in his own mountains victory over the invaders might well be a narrow, chancy business, and so he husbanded his fighters, seeing clearly that utter folly of frittering away irreplaceable strength in pointless harassment.

Next had come the refugees, trickling in first from the north, then from the south. At that point his control began to crumble away. Deep in his heart, he could not really blame the *dehrehbehee* and their tribesmen, for, had the situation been reversed, had he been a mere *dehrehbeh* with the sure knowledge that lowland raiders were ravaging Taishyuhn lands, he too would probably have led out his tribesmen to avenge former and prevent future inroads.

Nonetheless, with each departing tribe, his self-esteem eroded a bit more as he realized that his ability to stop the invading army became more questionable.

In sheer frustration, he beat his big fists against his muscular thighs. The cursed *brahbehrnuh* might well be right about her warriors and those of the Taishyuhns soon being the only fighters left here. But he vowed to himself, ere that happened, he would do *something*. If he could not stop the lowlanders here, he would at least dispose of the cursed Maidens. Maybe those tribes still with him could even fight or bluff their way into Maiden Valley and hold *it* against the Undying Devil.

None of the abashed *dehrehbehee* felt constrained to speak in the presence of the raging leader of their *stahn,* and in the silence of the familiar Council House, the *nahkhahrah* was able to muse on his problems undisturbed for some time. Then, as he had known it would, came an insistent pounding on the bolted door. From the sound, he imagined a sword pommel was being used on the polished hardwood.

Raising his chin from his chest, he calmly ordered, "Let the bitch in ere she splits the door. Or"—he smiled, the first smile any had seen light his seamed face in many a day—"has a tantrum and pisses her breeks."

In the blessed release from their long tension, the *dehrehbehee* all roared their laughter while one of their number pulled back the bolt and the *brahbehrnuh* swaggered into the dim, smoky room, trailed by her two guards, as ever.

Halting at the edge of their circle, she hissed at the council members, "You dare to laugh at the *brahbehrnuh* of Our Lady's Maidens?"

The smile instantly departed the *nahkhahrah's* countenance and his voice crackled coldly, like river ice. "We are the men who lead the Thirteen Tribes of the Ahrmehnee Stahn. We sit in council in our own council house and here we weep or shout or whisper or laugh whenever and as we please, asking leave of no man and, certainly, of no woman."

The *brahbehrnuh* stamped her foot petulantly. "I am your ally; it is the will of Her that I am your ally, and you have no right to deny me access to your councils. How do you expect me to hear what you dirty men are hatching when the door is barred against my entry?"

The *nahkhahrah* nodded slowly, the lamps making the shadows of his big-nosed, craggy face resemble the physiognomy of a bird of prey. "Yes, you are an ally, and only because it is Her will. But though it has been used as such in times past, this is not a true warhouse, it is the house of council for the business of the Thirteen Tribes of the Ahrmehnee. As you have obviously learned, its walls and door are thick and it has no windows for the very purpose of preventing spying and eavesdropping by curious busybodies and—"

But the armored woman burst out in interruption. "*Busybody?* Why you antique, tuskless boarhog, how *dare* you!"

His hours of meditation and other mental exercises had purged the *nahkhahrah* of anger, nor could her discourtesies and insults inflame him anew. "—and any others who would pry into matters which concern them not. I and my *dehrehbehee* and warriors are not of your valley or customs, so you have no right to know what is in our minds or of what matters we converse in privacy.

"Now, begone, child. Remain in your camp until I summon you, for I must journey with Our Lady this night." On his last words, he arose and pointed a long finger at the still open door.

A hot retort was on the *brahbehrnuh's* lips, but it never emerged. For all at once, the *nahkhahrah's* eyes locked with her own and the tall old man became even taller, larger, huger than any man had a right to be. It seemed this his white-haired head was truly brushing the sooty skull-bedecked rafters high above, that the width of his shoulders strained against the side walls of the council house. And the *brahbehrnuh* whirled and almost ran from the place now resounding with the contrabasso booming of the giant's voice.

With the rising of moon, the staccato voices of the *doombehgs* sounded from within the council house with, now and again, the lost-soul wailing of the reed-flutes rising above. Solid ranks of Ahrmehnee warriors—grim-faced and purposeful, firmly grasping their spears, darts and bared raider knives—barred any approach to the building. Those Maidens sent by the *brahbehrnuh* to inquire were told only that the *nahkhahrah* was in communion with the Holy Goddess and that, should their leader's presence be required, she would be summoned. No amount of insulting harassment or imperious demands could elicit the women any further information, and those few who sought to force a way through the ranks were either faced with a hedge of sharp and ready steel or hurled back to sprawl before the determined men.

All the *brahbehrnuh's* emissaries returned with bruised pride, some with bruised flesh as well, and at least one with a bloody nose. Hot words were screeched in the tent of the *brahbehrnuh*, the other Maiden leaders all being for arming and hacking a gory path through the insolent pigs who denied them their way. No one of them had ever before been denied anything by a mere man, nor had any man ever laid hand to them without being made to suffer for the outrage. But the *brahbehrnuh*, too, denied them.

Inside the council house, the noise was deafening. The air was thick and close with the heat of many braziers and with the pungent smoke of the herbs and gums regularly heaped upon the coals. Except for the braziers, all furniture had been removed, and the *nahkhahrah* and the *dehrehbehee* squatted in a circle in the center of the main room, while the drummers and other musicians crouched along the walls.

Though all had, of course, heard of it, only the older men had ever before been present when their chief of chiefs communed with the Lady. Despite their total nudity, those in the circle all were sweating heavily and quaffing deeply of the brimming bowls of barley beer. They had all fasted until an hour before moonrise, when each had consumed as much of the foul-tasting Holy Herb as he could force down.

None of them now were aware of the dozen warriors who silently glided to and fro, keeping the braziers fed and heaped, seeing that the beer bowls remained full and trimming the lampwicks.

As Moon rose higher and higher in the clear, cold sky, the drums roared on and on, the flutes keened and shrilled and the smoke roiled and billowed about the rapt circle.

At a signal from the *nahkhahrah*, someone outside placed before him a large silver bowl, its rim all chased with mystical and holy signs. Placing it beneath him, he urinated into it, then passed it to *Dehrehbeh* Neeshahn Soormehlyuhn on his left, who solemnly added the contents of his own bladder to the bowl, then handed the container to the *dehrehbeh* at his own left hand.

When all the circle had voided their water into the bowl, the *nahkhahrah* placed it before him on the floor, dipped out a half of a smaller bowlful and added an equal quantity of beer, then raised the smaller bowl to his lips and drained it off. Thrice more he did this, ere, a halfhour later, he slid from his place in the circle, and extended his body full-length upon the floor.

He closed his heavy lids.

"Once again, my faithful and ever-obedient son travels my way with me. Welcome and thrice welcome, Kohg Taishyuhn. What would you of Her who loves you?"

As he recalled from before, the unbearably sweet voice was all about the *nahkhahrah*, all about him and within him. And he opened his eyes to once more behold the unearthly beauty and splendor of the Lady. All of silver, She was. A soft and misty silver She glowed before and about him.

Then She no longer was all-encompassing, but—again, as before—a creature no taller than himself. A lissome, silver-haired, woman-shaped goddess, She was become.

She opened her slender arms to him and he entered into
Her embrace and he found Her silver-hued flesh cool and
pleasing to the touch and the scent of Her was redolent of
Moon-washed hills thick-grown with wild thyme. Their lips
met, locked, and Her kiss was cold fire, consuming all his
being, leaving nought behind save the aroused and stiffening ardor of his loins.

And when he had worshiped in the manner She desired,
when his loins had freely poured out a measure of their
most precious offering, then did the two arise from the billowy, silver couch and stroll, hand in hand, across the
springy, silver-bladed turf, to where a silver fountain
plashed misty silver water. They sat down on the cool
stone verge of the basin—all white marble, veined with the
Holy Silver.

She spoke. *"Dearest Kohg, the future of your people
can be far brighter than you and other mortals now believe. Once more will I allow you to spy out those places
and people and events which will shape the good and the
ill.*

*"I need not instruct you, for you have done this before.
Observe the past; see or be one with the present, as you
desire; then descry the futures which lie ahead and choose
the one you think best for your people . . . our people.*

*"When, at last, you are done, return to me and I will
again send you home.*

"Go you, now, loved lover."

Beneath his hurtling body, the night-cloaked mountains
rushed by. The *nahkhahrah* saw twinkling lights ahead,
swooped lower and recognized his village and the jagged
sprawl of camps surrounding it. He swept on, eastward,
over the range which lay between the village and the
wind-scoured, flinty waste of the Great Plateau. He
blinked in amazement when he saw the huge stone-and-
timber fort now rising above the icy plain. It had been reported to him, naturally, by his scouts, but they had failed
to impress him with the awesome size and strength of the
defenses. Even without wishing a glimpse of the possible
outcome, he dismissed all thoughts of hurling his
Ahrmehnee against those stout, well-manned walls.

Veering to his left, he plunged northward. Only a few
days' ride from his village, thousands of lowland cavalry
slumbered in and around a deserted village. A day behind
them, wild creatures scuttled about a battlefield, crouching

upon stiff Ahrmehnee corpses and gorging themselves on cold human flesh. And farther north lay horror upon horror of burned villages; the dead—or what the ravenous scavengers had left of them—lay thickly sown and living folk huddled, shivering, in the inhospitable mountains.

Turning about, the *nahkhahrah* bore to the south. Here, the camped lowlanders were not in one place, but in many, widely scattered. Behind them, forty miles wide, lay a swath of death amid ashes and ruin. The carnage had been fearsome here, and the destruction far more total than that to the north.

"He who wrought this," the *nahkhahrah* thought, "must be truly a monster of the Ancient Evil."

"*Monsters of the Ancient Evil are assuredly abroad in these mountains.*" Her voice once more enveloped him. "*But he who despoiled these, your folk, is not one of them, dear Kohg.*"

Recalling his plan to seize the Valley of the Maidens, the *nahkhahrah* bore about to the northwestward and, presently, he was gliding above the battlemented hills and ridges into a bank of noisome mist. From under the mist shone an eerie, roseate glow. The glow was strongest near the center of the largest vale, and he swept toward it. The air in the valley was warm, almost hot, and as he approached the source of that rosy radiance, the heat increased manyfold.

Something warned him to not come any closer to his objective, so he dove through the mist just shy of a huge fissure in the rocks. It belched forth a steady column of smoke and stench which brought tears to the eyes and acute discomfort to the skin. Waves of unbearable heat battered at him, and he blinked himself away. The clear menace of that fissure sent a shudder coursing through him.

Rising swiftly, he blinked the future, six moons ahead, and saw a scene of utter desolation. Tumbled rocks surrounded a wide bowl of bubbling, smoking almost-liquid. Nowhere was there any sign of a living creature.

"But . . . but, Lady? How? Why?" he begged silently.

And he felt himself whisked back to the present. Out of the yawning mouth of the entry cavern filed a long line of pack animals. Some bore strange devices strapped upon their backs, others, panniers which he could sense contained gold and silver, tons of the precious metals. The train was guided by strange-looking men and women in stranger garments. At its head rode three he recognized: the People-of-Powers. And though they spoke in a language he knew he had never heard, he could understand them.

"You're dead certain the charges will do what we planned?" queried Dr. Erica Arenstein anxiously. "Those that the gas didn't kill, those who only got a whiff of it, are going to be rather angry when they waken and find they've been robbed."

The Ahrmehnee-looking man who rode on her left snorted derisively. "Scant need of fear from that quarter, my dear Erica. Every last horse in their herd is presently roaming about these mountains, if not still running."

"Don't be suicidally cocksure, Dr. Corbett," the woman admonished him. "They are a stubborn race. If need be, they'll track us on foot, and unless we can get better speed out of these damned mules than we got in bringing them north, we'll be run down within a day's ride of here."

"Not to worry, honey," assured the other Ahrmehnee, him to whom she had first spoken, now riding a bit behind as the trail had become too narrow for three abreast. He glanced at an odd bracelet on his left wrist, then stated, "The tunnel will be sealed in thirty-two minutes, and before any of them—or many of them, at least—can climb up through those caverns and go down the walls, the main charges will blow. But by that time, we'll have that mountain yonder between us and the volcano. I calculate that the charges I planted will be just enough to trigger a full-scale eruption."

The woman, whom the *nahkhahrah* had known as Sahrah Sahrohyuhn, threw back her head and laughed merrily . . . and the *nahkhahrah* thought that never had he heard a more chilling sound.

"There, Kohg Taishyuhn, ride those you would term 'monsters.' "

"But . . . but, Lady, they are of You. They possess Powers."

"Poor mortal Kohg, you have been deceived. Those are not of Me. They are of a cankering sore upon the face of the troubled land. They and their kind honor not Gods but, rather, an abstraction they call 'Science.' Long, long ago, when untold millions of the races of man had forsaken the Gods to grovel at the altars of Science, the mon-

*strous creations of that false god almost swept the lands
clean of human life. Your people know of this through the
tales of 'The War of the Earth-Gods' and 'The Great Catastrophe,' Kohg.*

"*Few men survived the holocaust. Even today, the lands
are peopled by but a bare shadow of the numbers on
whom I once shed My rays. These Ancient Monsters move
and breathe only through an unspeakable perversion of the
Laws of Nature. And their future objective is nothing less
than the enslavement of all other living creatures. Not
many recognize the menace they present, Kohg, and one
who does is him they would have had you make war
upon, him you call 'Undying Devil,' him who calls himself, 'Milo Morai, High Lord of the Confederation.'* "

"But, the Devil is my enemy," protested the
nahkhahrah. "He drove my people from our rich lands,
drove us into these mountains, and now have his folk
soaked the earth with Ahrmehnee blood yet again. He is
Your enemy, as well, Lady. He worships Your enemy,
Sun."

The Voice remained cool and soothing in and about
him. "*He is not My enemy. Dear Kohg, I am all true
Gods. I but appear to men in the guise they venerate and
expect. To you, I am Moon Goddess, to Milo, am I God
of Sun and Wind; some call That which is Me Steel or
Rain; in the north I am worshiped as Blue Lady; even farther north, in the Black lands, men call upon Me as
Ahláh.*

"*Nor is Milo your enemy, Kohg. For even as all Gods
are but Me, the encompassing One, so too are all men of
all races brothers, could you poor mortals but see Truth.
Milo attacked your people and seized their lands principally to shorten his border and so protect his people from
your raiders. It is his aim to once more unite the lands
and races upon this continent—not as slaves beneath his
heel, such as would those whom you overheard, but as
free, happy and prosperous folk.*

"*Does this man—for, man he is; mortal man born of
woman, for all that some name him 'god'—succeed, does
he choose the proper combination of alternatives, as little
as seven thousand moons may see this land once again as
great and mighty as it was twelve thousand moons agone.*

"*This Milo is only your enemy because first your forefa-
thers, then you, have made him such. If you and your folk*

choose to freely join with his Confederation, you will be welcomed and heaped with honors. If you choose to fight on I can see no future for the Ahrmehnee, save as scattered, homeless, wandering remnants of a race. But it is you who must now choose, Kohg."

The *nahkhahrah* blinked the future and found it just as the Lady had stated; small family groups of Ahrmehnee, thin and ragged, barely existing in caves and makeshift tents, while being hunted like beasts by the Muhkohee, who had taken over Ahrmehnee valleys and rebuilt the war-shattered villages. He did not stay, for this possible future was too terrible to long contemplate.

And again he went soaring over the moon-bathed mountains, north and east this time. Just beyond his own village, he came to ground. Unseen, he passed between the guards and entered the tent of the *brahbehrnuh*, finding the young woman alone. Slowly, before her frightened and wondering eyes, he blinked his form visible.

"Listen to me, child." The *brahbehrnuh* could see his lips move, shape the words. Nonetheless, they seemed more within her head than upon her ears. "Your home is no more, nor your folk. Those whom we knew as People-of-Powers and of Our Lady were not; rather were they Monsters of the Great and Ancient Evil. They it was who slew your folk and despoiled your treasure, then destroyed your hold by means of the smoking fissure.

"Now, they bear their ill-gotten booty south and west upon the backs of many mules. There be but few of them, child, less than a hundred. Avenging the murders of one's own folk is a Sacred Duty. At dawn you must arm your Maidens and ride. You will ride with Her blessing."

The *brahbehrnuh* was not without real courage even in so eerie a situation as this, and she resolutely gathered that courage. "How . . . how came you here, without my guards? And how know *you*, who are only a man, of the Hoofprint of the Goddess's Steed, that which you called 'smoking fissure'?"

"Child, child, how can I make you understand? This night I am as one with Her, I ride with Her across the skies and can see all that She sees. It is only through Her powers that you look now upon my likeness, for my body actually lies yonder, within the council house."

The *brahbehrnuh* shivered, despite herself. Then, "If you . . . if you are a . . . a part of Our Lady, I . . . will believe, will do all that you can say if . . . if . . . if you will tell me my name. Tell me my secret name, the name I chose when first I became *bahbehrnuh*, the name which not even my lover knows, the name I have silently whispered only to the Goddess at Her shrine."

The *nahkhahrah* smiled gently. "It is a beautiful name, child. It was the name of my dear mother. It is Rahksahnah."

All the blood drained from the *brahbehrnuh*'s face, her strong legs wobbled, and only her grasp upon the table kept her from falling. She tried to speak, but could only gasp and stutter. Then, finally, she found her voice, though it was as weak as her body.

"I believe. It shall be as you, as She commands. The Maidens will ride at dawn."

The *nahkhahrah* briefly flickered out, then reappeared to add, "Pass wide of what was your home, Rahksahnah. The entrance now is sealed. To scale the heights and climb the walls would only be to die. And you must not die, for, ere you see my village again, you will find him who will make of you a true woman, give you a future of happiness and ease and children.

"I sense rebellion in your heart, child. Expel it. You must realize that the old ways of the Maidens are dead this night, dead and buried as the land which spawned you all will soon be. You must forget the past and accept the newness of the future, if you are to survive.

"Now I must leave you, for there is still much I must do ere the Lady complete Her journey."

Again the *nahkhahrah* swooped east. Over the range to the Great Plateau, then high over the expanse of sere grasses and frozen, rocky soil to the newly raised ramparts—raw earth and green logs and ancient blocks of stone. Unseen, he stood upon the wallwalk while an officer made his rounds. The block of granite beside the *nahkhahrah* once had been polished and engraved and it still bore ancient letters: *NAL BANK OF*.

He blinked. He saw the whole of the building of which the stone had once been a part, saw the other buildings about it, saw the odd folk who walked and talked and laughed and ate and loved, saw their black roads striped with yellow and white. He saw the folk conveyed upon their roads in large and small magical wagons, which made fearsome noises and trailed smoke behind. He saw thousands of bright lights, of every conceivable color, shining boldly or flickering in and out of fantastical designs.

He blinked. He saw the buildings and the roads again, but gone were the folk, gone too were the lights. Few were the wagons and they obviously had lost their magic, for they sat smashed and torn and rusting upon the cracked, weed-springing roads. The buildings, also, were dirt-streaked, many were sagging, and their windows gaped like the eyesockets of the skulls in the council-house rafters.

He blinked. He saw the broken block, now forming a merlon atop the battlement of the lowlanders' fort. He and his folk had pastured goats and cattle on this plateau time out of mind without ever suspecting that a city of the Earth-Gods lay beneath their feet.

"You have not much longer, My love. Hurry, Kohg, for soon I must send you back."

Milo awakened all in a breath, his hand immediately seeking the familiar hilt of his pillow-sword. At the foot of his couch stood a tall old man, devoid of any clothing. The face, though seamed and wind-darkened, still was handsome and the unbowed, muscular body bore the scars of a warrior. A single glance at the set of the intelligent eyes and the big nose, hooked like a hawk's beak, told the High Lord the man's race.

"Ahrmehnee!" he breathed. "How the devil did you get in here, old man? What do you want? If you've come to slay me . . ."

The visitor shook his snowy mane. "I am aware that steel cannot harm you, Milo of Morai. I am Kohg Taishyuhn, the *nahkhahrah* of the Thirteen Tribes of the Ahrmehnee. I am come to seek peace with you and a place for my people in your Confederation."

Chapter VI

Thoheeks Bili of Morguhn felt the first tingling and relaxed his mind to allow for easier farspeak.

"Bili," beamed the High Lord, "our war with the Ahrmehnee is ended. Send word to all your columns to re-tire back to the trade road and return to Vawn through Baikuh. Take your own force and ride northwest. You are seeking a muletrain which is led by three of the Witchmen . . . well, one is a woman. If you meet a force of ar-mored, mounted Ahrmehnee women, do not be surprised; they're after the same quarry.

"I'd like to have at least one of the Witchfolk alive, but remember what I've told you of them and their wiles and take no chances. The treasure they carry belongs rightfully to the Ahrmehnee warrior women of whom I just spoke. They are all virgins but, forgiving them that, the man who's seeking a rich wife could scarcely do better to my way of thinking. By the by, Bili, the *brahbehrnuh*, their leader, is reputed to be a proud, long-legged, handsome creature named Rahksahnah. She is of a long-lived, gifted race and should throw good colts, many of them.

"As for the machines they carry, I would prefer that they be smashed or, better yet, dumped in some deep, swift river.

"You'll be far west, Bili, so it's possible you'll chance across Mehrikan-speaking barbarians called Muhkohee. They are sly, savage and treacherous, lad. Even the wild Ahrmehnee fear them, so beware.

"Sun and Wind keep you all, Bili. Come to the *nahkhahrah*'s village when you are done."

Vaskos Daiviz of Morguhn, commander of the city of Vawnpolis, looked briefly at the stiffening corpse and repressed a shudder with difficulty. A veteran of the al-most constant border wars of the Confederation, he was no stranger to terrible sights. Nor did a man make the ascent from common spearman to sub-strahteegos without being an exceedingly tough and thick-skinned soldier. And Vaskos was both. Nonetheless, this body and the two found last week had chilled him to the very marrow.

All three had been women, young women. But had neighbors or friends not reported them missing, there would have been no chance of ascertaining the identities of the cadavers. Whoever had butchered them had, in all three cases, used a knife to mutilate their faces so that not even their mothers would have known them. Nor were these horrors the worst, for, after all, wounds wrought by steel were an old and familiar story to the commander.

No, what sent the cold prickling to Vaskos' nape while nausea churned in his belly were the *other* enormities perpetrated by the killer or killers. From the knees to the necks, the poor women had been savagely flogged, front and back. And atop the welts and cuts of the whip were the crowning horrors—the tears and gouges of teeth, human teeth, which had gnawed at the victim like an animal, ripping away chunks of flesh.

After the discovery of the first grisly remains by an early-morning patrol, Vaskos had concluded that none save a maniac could have done such a thing. Therefore he had sought out the keepers of Myros the Mad. But Captain Danos and all six of his men had attested that the former *vahrohnos* of Deskati had remained locked in his windowless chamber throughout the entire night. And since members of Vaskos' own staff had heard the madman's howls from time to time during the questioned time period, he had no choice but to scratch the suspect from his mental list.

After the second murder, he had doubled the night patrols, even though that meant putting a sizable number of former rebels back under arms. But this morning's find had proved even those measures ineffective. So he called his officers into council, inviting as well the few remaining former rebel officers: Captain Kahrlos, Captain Danos and *Vahrohneeskos* Kahzos Boorsohthehpsees of Vawn, once deputy commander of the rebel city.

It was the half-blinded and hideously disfigured young Ehleen nobleman to whom Vaskos addressed himself after he had succinctly reported the particulars of this most recent killing.

"Lord Kahzos, we must find a way to put a stop to these deaths, and since the victims are invariably from among those who were your people, I felt that you and these other two officers might be able and willing to aid."

Kahzos nodded gravely. He had given up his once-ready smile since he now smiled perpetually. A catapult stone had struck a merlon during the siege and the resultant hail of stoneshards had taken his left eye and grated all the flesh from the left side of his face.

"I don't think that it's a new problem, Lord Vaskos. Similar cases were noted by Lord Drehkos and me during the siege, as well as just preceding it. Always the victims were young women and girls, always were their bodies monstrously mutilated and showing marks of teeth. But after the first few weeks of the siege, the murders sort of . . . well, tapered off. These are the first sign that the murderer or murderers were not, as we had surmised and hoped, dead in the siege."

Vaskos sighed gustily. "My sincere thanks, Lord Kahzos. That takes quite a load off my mind. I was fearful that one or more of my Confederation garrison might have been culpable.

"Well, gentlemen, this narrows the field a bit for us. To narrow it further, we can eliminate those men who were on patrol last night as well as those who were known to be here in the citadel.

"I am posting a reward of one hundred silver *thrahkme-hee* for any information leading to the apprehension of this animal. *Eepohlohkahgos* Lain, you and your detachment will have the task of running down any leads and tips that that reward offer brings in. It might also be a good idea to incorporate some of our late enemies into your operation. I'm certain that Lord Kahzos would be happy to give you the names of some reliable men, and the Vawnee may find it easier to really open up to a fellow reb—uhhh, Ehleen."

The *vahrohneeskos* agreed with alacrity. "I certainly would. *Eepohlohkahgos*, I can have a number of men report to your offices and you then can pick and choose those with whom you feel you can best work. In fact, I myself am at your disposal. I want to see this criminal on a sharp stake as much as any here."

"My Lord Vaskos," put in Captain Kahrlos, leader of those former rebels now back under arms, "I'd 'preciate a part in this here, too. Y'see, it was a young widder, back las' fall, an' me an' her we was kinda close. She was a real fine woman an' . . . then one mornin' they foun' her poor body, what was left of it, leastways, in a alley oft High Street. I wouln' of knowed it was her, hadna been she had six toes on her feet. We . . . we was so happy, 'spite of the siege an' all. It'd do my soul good to hear the bastard what done all them things to my Aida scream fer a few days!"

Vaskos gave a brusque nod. "Of course, captain, you may take as much part in these proceedings as your duty allows. Speaking of which, I'm going to want a fifty-percent increase in the size of your force. See to it. As before, I cannot allow you to commission any officers, but you may appoint as many sergeants as you have need for."

Captain Danos, warder of the mad *vahrohnos*, Myros, listened intently to all that was said but offered neither aid nor advice. Since his responsibility and that of his small detachment was his charge, day and night every day, and since all knew him to be thoroughly dedicated to that responsibility, which had been his even before the siege had commenced, no one really expected him to tender the services of his six men in any other capacity.

For himself, Vaskos Daiviz was vastly relieved that the captain—formerly a hunter on the estate of the commander's father, *Komees* Hari Daiviz of Morguhn—was keeping his mouth shut, for it would be almost the final straw were he to find himself in any way beholden to the rebel officer. The stocky, powerful heir of Daiviz had but to finger the bumpy scar tissue just over his left ear, under the iron-gray hair, to recall that this same Danos had been a leader of the pack of rebels who had earnestly attempted to murder him last spring. They had slain Vaskos' orderly, brave Frahnkos, and had, like the houndpack they were, driven him and his three half-sisters from their home.

When, last summer, he and his father, with a mixed force of Freefighters and Confederation *kahtahfrahktoee,* had ridden back into Horse County and retaken their hall, this Danos had escaped the retributive bloodbath. Until the fall of Vawnpolis, none in the loyal forces had known the former hunter's fate or whereabouts.

Vaskos, then a supernumerary on the staff of the High Lord, had found the remembered name among the list of rebel officers turned in by *Vahrohneeskos* Drehkos Daiviz of Morguhn, his hated uncle. He and his father had then demanded an audience with the High Lord, recited the long list of Danos' crimes in Morguhn, and claimed the miscreant's blood . . . all of it. The High Lord had only promised to investigate the matter, pointing out, however, that the amnesty extended to *all* the former rebels and covered almost every crime they might have committed while in rebellion.

When he had given Vaskos command of the city and the attached base of operations for the mountain campaign, the High Lord had covered the case of Danos in his verbal orders.

"Vaskos, you're now a sub-*strahteegos*, but a responsibility such as I am placing in your hands is—or, rightfully, should be—that of a full *strahteegos*. Therefore, I am breveting you to that rank. Do a good job in Vawnpolis, and the end of this campaign will see the brevet rank a permanent rank."

Then, while the officer glowed with the promise of unexpected promotion, the High Lord had elucidated, where necessary, the written orders and added certain others. Lastly, he had added, "And, regarding this business which you and Lord Hari spoke with me about, this Captain Danos may well be everything of which you two accused him, and more. But he also was a brave and resourceful soldier, and his former commander, Lord Drehkos, has only the highest praise for him. Too, he is presently fulfilling a most valuable function in the city. I feel that he should continue in that function and in his current rank, at least until we've scotched these Ahrmehnee and Witchmen.

"As commander of Vawnpolis, you will find yourself working with and for the former rebels, and I expect you to get along well with them, all of them, including Captain Danos. Do I make myself clear, *Strahteegos* Daiviz?"

There had been no option and Vaskos had given the expected answer. Nonetheless, he had found it most difficult to be barely civil to this hated subordinate. He still did.

Not that he was too stiff-necked to give the devil his due. No man in the garrison or the city envied the captain his job. *Vahrohnos* Myros' madness was unpredictable and he could be extremely dangerous. Indeed, in one of his ragings, the lunatic had virtually torn limb from limb the sergeant who had originally been assigned to assist Danos.

At one moment, Myros would be the very epitome of the old-fashioned Ehleen gentleman—cool, poised, a bit arrogant, conversing in cultured accents—then, in a twinkling, he could become a ravening, blood-hungry beast with the strength of a wild bull and the murderous cunning of a treecat. Or, just as quickly, he could lapse into a coma from which he might not awaken for days or even a week.

In his day, the madman had been justly renowned as a master swordsman, and his keepers had early learned the folly of allowing their charge access to steel, no matter how pacific his mood might seem. No less than two men ever attended him, and they always carried long, leather, sausage-shaped cudgels rather than swords or dirks. Nor were they reticent in the use of their weapons when it became necessary to subdue the unfortunate nobleman. And Myros' battered physiognomy bore mute witness to his warders' self-protective impulses.

Soon after the close of Vaskos' meeting, Captain Danos sauntered down a hallway of the Citadel toward a thick, ironbound door, before which squatted a brace of armored men. Their helms laid aside, both were peering intently at the dice one had just cast.

The officer began to speak before he was well up to the pair. "Still at it, eh? Tell me, Sawl, how much does Geedos owe you by now?"

Fingering the place where his right ear—bitten off by Myros—had once sprouted, the brawny, thick-bodied man squinted his eyes and answered, "Well, cap'n, near as I can figure, 'bout twenty-three million *thrahkmehee*, give 'r take a couple of million." He added a gaptoothed grin.

Halting before the still-squatting men, Danos removed the sword from his baldric and the dirk from his belt and stooped to lay them by the two helms. Casually, he helped himself to one of the heavy, loaded cudgels, tightening its thong on his right wrist. Leaning over the gamesters, he slid back a brass panel and gazed through a grilled aperture into the chamber beyond, then slid the panel shut and stepped back.

"Open the door, Sawl. Geedos, make sure his lordship is on short chain. I wish to talk privately with him for a while."

When the officer entered his cell, Myros laid aside the book he had been reading by light of the two wall lamps which were kept constantly burning, well out of his reach.

A sneer twisted his lips as he suffered the guard to lift his feet onto the bed and shorten the chain which secured his left ankle to a finger-thick iron eyebolt let into the granite-block wall.

Few of the noble rebels now rotting in the prison at Morguhnpolis would have recognized the prisoner as the carefully groomed, satanically handsome man who had masterminded and led the rebellion in Morguhn. Blacknailed, filthy, clawlike hands poked from the sleeves of his stained and tattered shirt. The trimmed and oiled black mustachios and chinbeard of old now were merged and lost forever within the matted, gray tangle of whiskers which hung almost to his waist. His hair was almost totally white, as full and filth-matted as the beard. Even his fine, patrician nose had been knocked askew in one of the murderous set-tos with his "guards."

Only his glittering black eyes were unchanged, and from them his madness shone clearly. And something else peeked out as well, now and again; something which smacked to Danos, each time he chanced to see it, of dark, sinister, eldritch evil, which could see to the very core of his soul.

When the guard had adjusted the chain and left, closing the door behind him, Danos waited unspeaking until the muted clatter of the dice came from the hallway. Only then did he draw nearer and speak in hushed tones.

"My lord, I'll not be bringing you any more 'delicacies' for a while . . . possibly, a great while. The streets are going to be swarming with men every night for some time to come and it'll be just too risky to chance."

The *vahrohnos* showed his stained and broken teeth in a lazy smile. "You are lying, you whoreson. Vaskos-the-bastard hasn't enough of a garrison to mount a really effective guard, and I doubt me, with the sweet smell of *strahteegos* in his swinish nose, that he'll appeal for more men. So don't attempt to hoodwink *me*, you lowborn lout.

"How would you like me to start screaming for you, you personally, one night when you're out about your rather peculiar diversions, eh? How would you like for me to tell them exactly where to find you, under those ruins at the northeast corner of . . . ! *That* shook you, didn't it, captain?"

Pale and trembling, his quaking legs scarcely able to support him, Danos had backed as far from his demonic charge as he could. He leaned weakly against the wall, his nape prickling, while drops of cold fear oozed from his every pore.

The madman went on. "Oh, no, Danos, you'll continue to supply me my wants, for you are my prisoner as surely as I am yours. You'll bring me a quart of fresh blood at least twice each week, and I care not where or how you get it. Woman's blood or man's blood, it matters not. But you *will* bring me blood!"

Using the mind of Whitetip, his prairiecat, to boost his farspeak range, Bili bespoke those few minds with which he was familiar to alert four of his farflung squadrons to the High Lord's new orders. For the others, he sent out dispatch riders at dawn. Also at dawn, he divided his personal command, sending the four reserve squadrons back to the trade road in company with the mule-and-pony train of booty, the dozen or so wounded Freefighters and most of the supply train. When he spurred westward, it was at the head of a full squadron, made up of the best of five.

Noble and Freefighter, officer and man, they were, in appearance, a rather unprepossessing lot that chill morning. Nearly a month of unrelieved campaigning up through the inhospitable mountains had given them the look of ruffians—mostly unwashed, untrimmed and unshaven, showy with gaudy bits of looted Ahrmehnee finery, acrawl with vermin. Albeit, there were few glum faces among them, and for two principal reasons: first, they had encountered few warriors and had consequently suffered few casualties; second, the pickings of the villages had been good, better than most had expected of mountain barbarians, and every rider who arrived back below the walls of Vawnpolis was assured of a jingling share of the loot now being packed south on the long trains of mules and asses and "liberated" mountain ponies.

But, for all their appalling personal hygiene, or lack of same, all their weapons were honed and bright, their armor rust-free and well oiled. Saddles and other leather gear were supple and shining, and every horse was in the best possible condition.

Pleased as the mercenaries were with the ease and profits of this campaign, they were even better pleased with their young commander, Duke Bili. Too often, within the borders of the Confederation, they had been forced to sell their swords to southern nobles who basically disliked, if not openly despised, Freefighters. But this tall, stark warrior whose Red Eagle banner they now followed not only liked and respected them, he understood them and their customs, shared their grim religion and spoke their language.

Confederation-born, of mixed Ehleen and Horseclans paternity, his dam a daughter of the Duke of Zunburk, he was less than a year come down from the court and many battlefields of the Iron King, speaking the nasal Harzburker dialect better thaan he spoke Ehleeneehkos. Even his Confederation-Mehrikan was tinged with a northern accent which, to the Freefighters, gave his orders a homey sound. Reared amongst northern nobles, he behaved like them, which fact often enraged his Kindred and Ehleen subordinates, but further endeared him to the northern mercenaries, who willingly rendered him the honors due a burk-lord and referred to him fondly as "Duke Bili the Axe."

Depending on Whitetip, the long-fanged prairie cat, ranging out ahead of the column, to sniff out any ambuscades and farspeak to him of them, as well as on his own rare ability to foresense danger, Bili rode easily, slouched against the high cantle of his warkak. Long inured to the harsher clime of the north, he and most of the Freefighters had suffered less from the rigors of the winter-gripped mountains than had many of the Kindred nobility. And this was one reason he had so few of the latter with him now. Another reason was their inborn penchant for arguing the most minor details of orders under any and all conditions.

It had come as a distinct shock to Bili—and to his brothers too, who, like him, had been reared in various of the Middle Kingdom principalities—that even untitled, minor nobility of the Confederation felt not only free but almost constrained to argue the decisions and commands of major nobles, right up to their own, hereditary lieges. A northern knight or baronet or even the lord of a small burk who took it into his head to do such would part company with that head, and right speedily, too.

And their constant complaints about the rigors and discomforts of camp and march and campaign were not the mumbled grousing expected of all soldiers, but formal protestations, delivered personally and at maddening length. It had been bad enough during the siege of Vawnpolis, when the most unstinting of the bellyachers could be sent packing, sent on one pretext or another back to their desmesnes, ere their big, active mouths undermined both morale and discipline. But on this present campaign, only large, well-armed bodies could be sent back through the ravaged and highly vengeful tribal lands, so Bili had found himself stuck with a large minority of long-overindulged men who considered themselves his peers and who often behaved as if it was his fault that it was too cold or too wet for their pampered tastes.

Bili had long been proud of his iron control over his hot temper, but these Kindred nobles had driven him to distraction, and it had frequently been all he could do to keep from blooding his axe or sword on their miserable necks. Therefore, he had considered it the bountiful blessing of Sun and Wind to rid himself of all the whiners ere setting forth on this mission to the west. And their howls of protest when he had commandeered their well-schooled warhorses and vastly superior armor for certain of his Freefighters had been sweet to his ears.

Those few Kindred who now rode west with him were either atypical younger men who had quickly and easily adapted to northern modes or older nobles who had, in their salad days, soldiered in the Middle Kingdoms as free lances. Few were his actual liegemen—Morguhn or Daiviz Kindred—but he had come to love them like brothers. One such, *Komees* Taros Duhnbahr of Baikuh, rode knee to knee with him.

Born a third son, Taros had never expected to succeed to his father's title and lands, but, two days after his twenty-second birthday, the former *komees* and both the elder brothers had been slain in that last attack against the walls of Vawnpolis. Their smoke was not half a day with Wind, before *Thoheeks* Baikuh had confirmed Taros to possession of his patrimony. Even yet, he sometimes seemed startled when addressed as *komees* or *count*.

"Lord Bili," he said respectfully, "I can truly understand why you sent back those querulous old women and precious young Ehleenee, but you know there's going to be merry hell to pay if any of their horses are lost or any of their plate either. Aren't you worried about starting bloodfeuds?"

"With such as them?" Bili's white teeth sparkled in a

brief, humorless grin. "Hardly. Had they any gumption, they'd have given me the same answer Veetos of Lahmahnt did, that where his horse and armor went, so too went his sword and his body. There's hope for a man that stubborn, no matter how delicate his manner or quarrelsome his nature."

At the midpoint of Sacred Sun's journey, they stopped long enough to chew Ahrmehnee-cured meat while the horses grazed on scant grasses and weeds, frost-sere and partially snow-covered. Then it was into the saddle and face the west again, following whatever tribe or game trails were available. Then the head of the column turned the flank of a wooded slope to see the track ahead blocked by a knot of armored and mounted warriors.

Signaling for a halt, Bili mindspoke Mahvros, his stallion, to a trot. Trailed by *Komees* Taros and the trooper who bore the Red Eagle of Morguhn, he advanced to exchange handclasps and greetings with the waiting nobles and officers.

Komees Hari Daiviz of Morguhn looked at least twenty years younger than he had on the day almost a year ago, when he had received Bili in his hall and the young *thoheeks* told him so.

Hari smiled broadly. "I'd forgotten just how much fun a protracted raid on hostile territory can be, Bili. And you won't believe how much loot we're sending south, either, not until you see the size of your tenth of it, you won't. Who'd have thought these wretched Ahrmehnee could've accumulated such wealth, up here away from everything?"

"Probably," mused Bili aloud, "they got most of it the same way they lost it, raiding the nearer duchies and the other mountain tribes. Have your losses been heavy?"

Hari shrugged. "Ten killed or dead of wounds, maybe thrice that hurt in one way or another, none so bad they couldn't sit a horse. But I fear that some of our columns may not have been so fortunate, Bili. A warhorse limped into camp, two nights back. The creature's mindspeak is minimal, so I wasn't able to get much information from him, but I'd have recognized him anyhow. It's Pawl Raikuh's gelding, Bili, and the saddle was caked with dried blood."

"Well," the *thoheeks* sighed, "Pawl would be the first to say that death is nothing more than the rest at the end of the long march. It's a rare soldier who finds it in a bed,

Hari. Let's just hope he died in battle, hope the damned Ahrmehnee didn't take him alive."

Hari's fingers sketched the Sun-sign. "Double aye to that! Not even on my . . . on the commander of Vawnpolis's rebels would I wish such a cruel fate."

Pehroosz Bahrohnyuhn had thought she would never spend so horrible a night as that which followed the day of her brutal violation. She had lain upon the greasy dirt floor, her stained cloak wrapped tightly about her bruised and aching young body, while the creatures of the mountain night snapped and snarled over the freezing carcasses of the butchered herd of goats and the corpses of her three little brothers. Carefully, she had husbanded the wood from the meager furnishings so senselessly smashed by the raiders who had raped her, fearful of letting the fire die completely but even more fearful of unlacing or raising the heavy hides which closed the open side of the herdmen's shelter and which were now all that separated her and Zahndrah, the old milkgoat, from the scavengers.

But after the endless dark had come the light of the new day. She had heard no more animal sounds for some time, so when Zahndrah commenced to paw and nibble at the hides, she found the courage to flex her stiffened limbs and crawl over. Recalling all too well the agonizing cramps which had racked her lower abdomen when, yesterday afternoon, she had tried to stand and walk, she followed the goat out on hands and knees.

But once in the sunlight, her pride took over. Since she had been gone from the village nearly twenty-four hours, it was certain that someone would soon come seeking her, especially with raiders about. It would not do for villagers to see her—naked but for her cloak and fur-lined boots—whimpering on her knees, no matter what injuries and degradations she had suffered. After all, she was eldest born to their *hetman.*

Gritting her teeth against the expected cramping and grasping the low lintel timber for added support, she pulled herself to her feet. However, after a brief stab or two, the internal pain subsided to but a gnawing discomfort, unpleasant but bearable. That was when she became fully aware of her other pains. Worst was the tender flesh at the base of her belly, smarting as if red-hot irons had been pressed against it.

But the most serious of her injuries appeared to be to her hands. The raider who had knelt on her palms, while his comrades had had their vicious sport of her body, had rested the full weight of his body as well as that of his armor. Now, after a night of stiffening she had but minimal use of her fingers, and the pain which shot up her arms when she tried to close the hands enough to really grip the lintel brought beads of sweat to her forehead and a low moan bubbling from her lips.

So, before trudging back toward the village, she made her painful way up the near slope of the intervening mountain. Clad only in cloak and boots as she was, she shivered almost constantly as the chill increased, and her teeth chattered as she wove her way between clumps of evergreens. But at last, she was before the dark opening of the cave of the Woman of Wisdom, Zehpoor.

So long as Ahrmehnee had dwelt in the nearby valley this cave had been the abode of a Woman of Wisdom. Many said that this same one had been here since the time of the Earth-Gods; others, that she was but the latest in a succession of such healer-priestesses. Pehroosz could not say. She had seen Zehpoor but once—at the time when she and three other pubescent girls had been brought up to be admitted to the Women's Mysteries—and her only memory was of an ancient, frail and withered face mouthing incomprehensible words.

Shivering now as much from awe as from cold, Pehroosz haltingly entered the outer chamber, knelt reverently before the altar of the Lady, then leaned forward to press her lips against the Skystone.

"What would you, Pehroosz Bahrohnyuhn?" The words seemed to come from above, from below, from all about the small, stone room.

Pehroosz scarcely recognized her own voice, issuing from the throat screamed raw yesterday and the lips swollen from buffets and brutal, forced kisses.

"Oh, please, Mother Zehpoor, I have been . . . hurt. I . . . I need healing before I can go back home, back to the village."

After a moment, a slender column of smoke arose from a crack in the top of the small altar and that disembodied voice commanded, "Breathe you of the smoke, child. Breathe it deep, Pehroosz."

Obediently, the girl did so. All at once, the icy stone

beneath her knee became as warm as sun-baked rocks, the very air about her, balmy as summer. Gone was all pain, all discomfort, all remembered horror. Both body and mind seemed to be sinking slowly into soft, safe warmth. She closed her eyes, breathing a sigh of relief.

Chapter VII

Afterward, she could only recall a long period of waking slumber, wherein a formless blob of face flitted in to briefly float before her while hands pressed a bowl rim to her mouth and a half-heard voice urged her to drink substances ranging from nauseous and bitter to sweet and soothing. But, mostly, she simply floated, weightless, feeling nothing save comforting warmth.

At last, she opened her eyes unbidden. Above her, a ceiling of polished hardwood was almost obscured under untold layers of soot; beneath her body, she felt the warm softness of a feather mattress and, dimly, the feel of the rope supports. It was purest luxury. In the village, only her father's greatbed boasted so fine and thick a mattress.

"So," chuckled a remembered voice from her right, "my little chicken awakes at last."

The turning of her head brought to her eyes the sight of Mother Zehpoor. The crone sat in a carven chair before a heavy table, on which was a huge stone mortar, surrounded by bunches and bundles of dried herbs and roots. Gently dropping the pestle back into the mortar, she arose from her place and padded lightly over to plump herself down on the edge of the bed.

Seeing her at close range, Pehroosz was shocked. The Mother Zehpoor of the rites—less than sixty moons agone—had been ancient and withered, while this woman, though very slender, looked to be little older than Pehroosz's mother.

The woman's lip and eye corners crinkled. "Oh, but I am that same Mother Zehpoor, child. You and the others, you saw what you saw because I willed that you see it. My reasons for deceiving your sight rest between me and Her I serve.

"But come, let us see your hands, Pehroosz." Tenderly,

she commenced to unwrap the linen bandages. "The Lady grant they are at last healed, for we must soon begin our journey, if we are to fulfill Her will." She sighed. "It is almost a moon's ride to the place wherein fates will be cast."

"Journey?" Pehroosz interjected, wide-eyed. "Forgive me, Mother Zehpoor, but I don't think my own mother would . . . how long have I been here? Surely, I have been missed by now. Have none come to seek me?"

The woman's face became grave and sympathy shone from her sloe-black eyes. "Pehroosz Bahrohnyuhn, you are descended of brave warriors and wise chiefs; you are descended, moreover, of a proud and most ancient race. Much have the Ahrmehnee suffered, child, yet have their pride and their valor ever sustained them. As you well know, this is not our original *stahn*. The Horse-devils and the Enleenee now squat upon the fertile lands which once were ours. But—and this you may not know, Pehroosz— there were still other *stahns* from which we were driven, long, long ago, in the time of the Earth-Gods. Many moons' sail away, they lie, far across the Great Sea.

"Mighty were those *stahns*, large and powerful and very rich. But, corrupted by wealth, those ancient Ahrmehnee turned from adoration of the Lady to worship of other gods, false gods. From that moment did fortune depart from our race, Pehroosz. Race after race did harry and hound our ancestors, driving us from our lands and cities and villages, stealing our kine and our goods and our maidens. But, even in those dark times, did our inborn courage and pride bear us up.

"Your blood is as their blood, Pehroosz Bahrohnyuhn. You have suffered most cruelly. Now must I relate that which will cause you still more anguish, yet must you bear your woes as stoically as did your suffering ancestors, down through the ages."

Drawing a deep breath, she stared levelly into the girl's wide eyes. "Pehroosz, those men, the ones who attacked you, who butchered the goats and slew your brothers, were but part of a far larger raiding party. Only an hour after you were ravished, child, more than five hundred men assaulted the village. Those who escaped their cruelty fled northward. Those who did not lie dead among the ashes and tumbled stones.

"You may be as proud of your mother's memory as you

are of young Toorkohm's. She directed what pitiful defense could be made and fought as bravely as any warrior could've until she was cut down."

Abruptly, Pehroosz sat up and made to lower her feet to the floor. "Please, Mother Zehpoor. Please, we must bury my mother's body."

Firmly, the woman pushed her back down on the bed. "Pehroosz, you must not go to the place that was the village. It has been a long, hard winter, child, and game has been scarce. In the four days since the village was burned, the bears and the wolves, the treecats and smaller animals will have left very little of those folk slain there."

"But . . . but it cannot have been so long," protested Pehroosz. "I came to you only this morning."

The woman shook her head of tightly coiled, iron-gray hair. "Not so, child. In less than an hour, the sun will rise on the fourth morning you have been with me. I thought it best that you remain asleep while your body's hurts healed, that your mind not be forced to dwell upon the horrors you endured. But now you are once more hale and we must leave."

"But why, Mother Zehpoor? Why must we leave? This is my home and soon my father will return and rebuild the village. And . . . and Hahkeeg, too—we are to be married soon."

"Child," said the woman, patiently, "we must leave because it is the Lady's will. Whilst you slept, I did scry the future. To remain here is death. Far from here, far to the west, lies your fortune, Pehroosz—a fabulous dowry of long-hidden wealth, a strong and brave and gentle husband of another race who will give you a life of ease and comfort and will receive of you fine sons to bring fresh honors to his house and tribe. But we must leave soon and travel cautiously, for the mountains swarm with bands of lowlander raiders."

The woman arose and smoothed down her skirt. "So, come you, child. You must eat now. I have fawn seethed in goat's milk and oatcakes and honey wine. Then you must help me prepare for our journey. It is commanded that I go, too, for, somehow, my future is tied up to yours."

Quite early in his westward dash, Bili found it necessary

to place his command on meager field rations, since they were no longer assured of the superfluity of supplies which raiding brought. There was some grumbling, but most recognized the need to reserve the grain for the horses, who could not maintain their best form on the scant subsistence of the half-feral mountain ponies; not so, some of the young *thoheeks*'s more vocal, noble critics, however.

As he had progressed, as his path had crossed those of the fanned-out columns of raiders, Bili had rendezvoused with almost all of his Morguhn nobles and the survivors of the original Morguhn troop of Freefighters who had marched into Vawn under his banner. The majority, he had been glad to see again—his brothers, Djaik and Gilbuht, *Komees* Hari, Freefighter lieutenants Krahndahl and Hohguhn—others he would have been as happy to not see. Or hear.

They were, by now, within a few days' ride of their objective, the area wherein the High Lord had thought they should intercept the Witchmen and the booty train. Therefore, Bili had assembled most of the officers and nobles, that the High Lord's instructions be detailed to all. Along the twisting length of a narrow, steep-sided vale, the Freefighters were laying watchfires, setting up picket lines and caring for their horses; after nearly a week of sunrise-to-sunset forced marches, they were reveling in the unaccustomed luxury of having natural light by which to set up camp.

A cursory glance at his subordinates showed all the Morguhn nobles present with the sole exception of *Vahrohneeskos* Ahndros. Then, from the summit of the small mound on which he stood, Bili recognized the baronet's big gray gelding coming rapidly down the length of the vale. For all that the beast was already at full gallop, its rider could be seen to spur-rake the sweaty barrel, while lashing furiously with his crop.

Only good fortune prevented Ahndros' steed from tramping the soldiers in his path. Even as Bili watched, grim-faced, the rocketing destrier's shoulder took a Freefighter in the back, sending him spinning to the rocky ground with a mighty clashing of scale armor.

At the periphery of the gathering, the gelding was savagely reined to a shuddering halt. Stiff-legged, the *vahrohneeskos* stalked through the throng, directly toward the *thoheeks*. His saturnine countenance bespoke ill-concealed rage, his dark eyes smoldered, his right hand continually clenched and unclenched and the knuckles of his left hand gleamed white on his swordhilt. Shouldering through the front rank, he came to a halt and stood, spraddle-legged, before his suzerain.

Although he had not been with the column twenty-four hours, Ahndros had already found occasion to be publicly insubordinate, first to *Komees* Hari, then to Bili. Even a half-blind dolt could have seen another such outburst here aborning, and Bili was more perceptive than most. His eyes like blue ice and his voice as cold, he broke off his conversation with a Freefighter captain to ask:

"You have yet another complaint, baronet?"

In tones every bit as glacial, the newcomer replied, "*My* title is '*vahrohneeskos*,' my lord *thoheeks*. I am not one of your precious unwashed burk-lords! And I want to know why your damned barbarian baggage master refused to issue my cook a few pounds of grain to make flour for my bread. And what right did the lowborn swine have to jettison three packloads of my personal baggage and drive the ponies away from the march route? Who, just who do you think you are, you immature jackanapes? How much more of your supercilious contumely do you think I and the other Kindred gentlemen are going to tolerate? Only my love for your mother has restrained me ere this, but it's high time someone took you and your insufferable arrogance to task!"

Ahndros's face, blood-dark when he first began, had now become pallid with rage, and a patch of froth quivered at his lips' corners, while a tic twitched his cheek and eye.

Unmoving, grim-faced Bili heard out the enraged man. Those about the two perceptibly moved back, sensing an imminent combat. At Ahndros's last word, Bili broke his silence, sneering.

"Don't hide behind your supposed regard for one of my mothers, little man. If anyone's arrogance has made him insufferable since first he joined the siege forces, it is you, Ahndros Theftehros of—Sun and Wind help us all—Morguhn. I have never fully understood why you joined us at all, since you found my judgment, the High Lord's judgment, Aldora's judgment, all wanting. I have never given you an order that you didn't take exception to some part of, when you didn't disregard it altogether.

"So little actual combat did you take part in, at Vawnpolis, that I'd have had adequate reason to question your courage—as did certain of your peers—did I not know better. You fought with and for me against heavy odds last year, took grievous wounds in my service, and I am grateful. Because of that gratitude, I have been more than lenient, more than tolerant of your flagrant improprieties. But, no more, sirrah!

"I am not yours to command, rather you are mine. I am your hereditary lord, Ehleen. Moreover, I am in command of this column. We are on compaign in the midst of hostile country and I cannot—dare not—tolerate anything, man, cat, horse or object, that impedes our progress or endangers us or sows dissension amongst us. Therefore, I'll give you three choices: you can take the five servants you saw fit to bring, along with a small escort, and make your way back to your former posting, then lead them back to Vawnpolis; you can recognize your proper place and station and stay in it, physically and verbally; you can continue to comport yourself as previously and I'll have you executed as the troublemaker you are.

"Make your choice, Ahndros Theftehros. Now!"

Ahndros's full lips curled his scorn. "Even such a thing as you would not dare to slay me without a legal hearing before my peers of Morguhn. The High Lord would have *your* hairless head for such highhandedness, and you know it. Command your stinking barbarians, if you wish and can—you should be able to do that, anyway, since you're a savage, unlettered burk-lord in all save name, yourself!—but we noblemen, Kindred *and* Ehleenee, are your puppets only so long as we allow you to pull our strings. I, for one, have no intention of slavishly following your stupid whims, of allowing you to further humiliate me and deny me my lawful rights, nor will I allow you to degrade me by chasing me out of camp.

"So, since I flatly refuse two of your magnanimous offers and since we both know that you dare not carry out the third and, since you seem averse to meeting me honorably, as a gentleman should . . ." He allowed his voice to trail away, smiling lazily. Ahndros was easily the second-best swordsman in either Morguhn or Vawn—only Djaik

Morguhn possessed superior talent and skill with broad-sword or saber—so he was absolutely sure of his ground. Either Bili—hated Bili—would rise to the bait and become a corpse or he would not and lose the respect of all and the command of the column, which latter Ahndros himself craved.

While an officer in the Confederation Army, Ahndros had been lover to Aldora and an honored favorite of the High Lord. Even after he had succeeded to his father's title and lands and resigned his commission, he had been a person whom the High Lord contacted frequently, and he had been the only soul in all of Morguhn who had known that Milo would visit the duchy in the guise of a traveling bard. Consequently, it had come as an especially bitter pill to find, upon his recovery from wounds and joining of the army before Vawnpolis, that *Thoheeks* Bili had replaced him in both capacities.

Early on, he had found his relative lack of status un-bearable and had tried to rewin his former place with both High Lord and High Lady. He had failed miserably. To Aldora, unashamedly in love with Bili, Ahndros was just one more in the scores of former bedmates she had had over the century and a half she had lived. Milo, for his part, had come to admire, respect and love Bili in his own way; Bili's astounding mental abilities—not yet fully ex-plored or completely understood—his natural leadership and aptitude for inspiring his followers, his quick and ac-curate assessments of situations and problems, his personal valor and cleanly habits and blunt candor, all had impressed the High Lord.

Deep within himself, Ahndros had been able to under-stand, for he too had had an instant liking for the stark young warrior who had ridden down from the north to as-sume his patrimonial duties. Moreover, there was the link of shared combat and dangers, for he and Bili and the High Lord had held a bridge for almost an hour against a horde of mounted rebels. In that springtime skirmish had he taken the wounds which for so long had invalided him. Lastly, he lusted after one of Bili's mothers, the late *Thoheeks* Hwahruhn's eldest widow.

Even so, his sickening envy for the stations once his and now held by Bili soon blossomed into hate. Assiduous nitpicking produced no dearth of fuel for stoking the fires of that hate. Also, he found a willing fire tender in the person of old *Komees* Djeen Morguhn, whose earlier, overbearing efforts to browbeat Bili had ultimately resulted in his own public humiliation, an act for which he could never forgive his young overlord. Throughout the siege, these two had been able to cause Bili and Aldora—the High Lady having been left in charge of the besieging forces during the High Lord's lengthy absence—considerable annoyance and not a little real trouble.

Nonetheless, the habitual caution of the elderly *komees* had in some measure restrained Ahndros' less calculating nature from open and violent defiance. But *Komees* Djeen had been in command of the farthest-eastward squadron, and so was presently withdrawing with his force to the south. Ahndros was now completely on his incautious own.

Though Bili answered the barb as calmly as possible, it was from betwixt tightly clenched jaws, above which his eyes blazed blue fire. "When once more we are our own men, Lord Ahndros, without mission and orders and responsibilities for those we lead, you will find me more than happy to let Steel decide our differences. For the nonce, however, we are all under the High Lord's command to fulfill his behests, and, as I have before told you, we are far from the Confederation and in the midst of a hostile land. It was the High Lord's express wish that I captain this special enterprise, and I will not surrender that captaincy to you or anyone else without the Lord Milo's order.

"My farspeak summons to you instructed you to join this column at the specified rendezvous with a half-dozen troopers or officers and a bare minimum of equipment. Since we were to move far and fast, I said nothing about bodyservants, yet you appeared with five, plus a half-troop and a packtrain near as long as this entire squadron's. Tents and scents and oils and fine clothing have no place in the High Lord's plans, Lord Ahndros, nor in mine; this is why the baggagemaster dumped your three packloads, and I had intended to so inform you, though, for your pride's sake, I'd not have done so in public.

"The grain and dried beans are being retained to keep our warhorses in proper flesh, since, unlike the ponies, they cannot thrive on dry grass and treebark. Even the lowliest trooper seems to understand this, Lord Ahndros. Why can't you?"

During Bili's long reply, Ahndros' blood had cooled enough to allow his brain to register a few very important facts: Bili was not wearing a sword; it hung, along with his axe and helm, on the saddle of Mahvros, his black stallion, some paces to his rear. His sneer intensified and he hitched his swordbelt forward and closed his right hand about the wire-wound hilt.

"I don't think these noble gentlemen and northern officers are willing to follow the lead or orders of a craven, no matter his hereditary rank or who misplaced him in command." He raised his voice and glanced about him. "What say you, gentlemen? The *thoheeks* of Morguhn has done me injury, yet he refuses to meet me in honorable combat, and such refusal brands him craven. Do you now follow him or me?"

Lord Hari, his face fire-red, made to step forward, but Djaik Morguhn was there before him. "Lord Ahndros, I know not the customs and usages of the Confederation Army, but I had assumed it at least as civilized and well ordered a force as the armies of the Middle Kingdoms. In the Army of Eeree, now, a nobleman—no matter how high his birth—who saw fit to insult his commander, openly question that commander's judgment and tender a challenge which he knew the commander's oaths would not let him take up would be brought before a drumhead court-martial and, most probably, a Steel Cult Council, as well.

"The Order would likely bid him do combat with a weapons master in full plate and him with but a sword and his bare skin. If, by wildest chance, he survived that encounter—"

"*Fagh!*" Ahndros burst out. "Your barbarian practices would sicken a hog. Find someone else to yap at, puppy, I have business with grown men."

Grave-faced, the younger Morguhn turned to Bili. "Brother, I ask Sword-leave. Be it your will?"

At Bili's mindcall, Mahvros gave over his browsing and paced to Bili's side, his harness jingling. Feeling the super-charged emotional atmosphere, the sensitive horse mind-spoke with rising eagerness. "Do we fight soon, brother?"

"Not me, Mahvros, but possibly you with my brother, Djaik, astride you. Will you serve him as you would me?"

"My brother's brother is my brother," the horse answered simply.

Bili lifted his baldric from off the pommel, uncased the sword and dropped baldric and sheath to the ground. Turning back to Djaik and the assemblage, he raised the broadsword to his lips, kissing the blade just below the guard.

Djaik drew his own sword and did likewise, then he extended his hilt to Bili, accepting Bili's sword in return.

"No, not Sword-leave, my brother," stated Bili formally. "Rather, this. You are me, until my Steel runs lifeblood."

Stiffly, Djaik nodded. "I will serve your honor well, lord brother. Honor to Steel." Once more, the two men kissed their blades.

"What are you two yammering about?" shouted Ahndros, peevishly. "Is the craven *thoheeks* going to fight me or not?"

Still gripping Djaik's bare blade, Bili stalked forward, saying, "Count Hari, I beg you and Sir Geros attend and advise Lord Ahndros, as I doubt me he knows aught of Sword Cult usages."

Once again confronting Ahndros, Bili grounded the point of his brother's sword, crossing his big, scarred hands upon its pommel-ball. "You were insistent on a duel, eh? Well, a duel you are to have, sirrah. Were I free to do so, I'd meet you myself, on horseback, with axes. But I'm not, as you well know.

"However, Lord Ahndros, you have challenged and my surrogate has taken up that challenge. You will meet my brother, Djaik Morguhn, as soon as he has fully armed. It will be a combat conducted by Sword Cult customs, in which Count Hari and Sir Geros Lahvoheetos of Morguhn will presently instruct you.

"You have been most provocative, Lord Ahndros, but, even so, I would prefer reconciliation and comradeship to combat. Therefore, I offer you the opportunity to withdraw your challenge, apologize for your insults and rejoin us as a loyal and obedient Kinsman."

It was not working out as Ahndros had hoped. He did not really fear Djaik, though he respected the boy's unquestioned expertise, but he had no desire to fight him, nothing to gain in wounding or killing him, save the enmity of all of Clan Morguhn. He would have been happy to live with that enmity, could he only have hacked the life out of the *thoheeks*, but, once again, circumstances had conspired to cheat him of his rightful deserts. Utter frustration was compounded with his rage and the mixture suddenly bubbled over, completely out of control.

His sword sang clear of its scabbard, flashing blindingly in the westering sun. *"Christ damn you, you heathen bastard*! It's not your brother's blood I want, it's yours. You've got a sword. *Use it!"* And with that he stamped forward, his forehand slash aimed at Bili's helmless head.

Chapter VIII

Ahndros should have known better; he had, after all,
seen Bili fight. For all his thick waist and hips almost as
wide as his shoulders, the young *thoheeks* was in no manner clumsy or slow, else he would not have lived through
over five years of almost continuous warfare. His quick re-
flexes had saved his life in more than one fierce encounter.
They did again.

Experience told him that he could not get the long,
heavy sword up quickly enough to effectively parry the attack. To duck would only make him more vulnerable, and
to hop back off the small mound would be to give
Ahndros the advantage of high ground. Dropping the
sword, he threw himself forward, his meaty shoulder striking the center of Ahndros' breastplate, his left hand closing on his adversary's right wrist with bone-crushing force.

Ahndros crashed over backward, his cuirass striking
sparks from the rocky ground. They rolled over and over,
the gathered men scattering from their path. The fall had
sent Ahndros' helm spinning, but Bili could not spare a fist
to batter the exposed head or fingers to gouge the eyes or
ram up the nostrils, for he needs must use both hands to
protect himself from Ahndros' strength.

Cursing in all the languages or dialects he had ever
heard, *Komees* Hari danced about as close to the com-
batants as their unpredictable writhings would permit, his
blade bared, seeking a safe opening through which to
thrust or slice some unarmored portion of Ahndros' anat-
omy.

As for Ahndros, he knew that to release his grip on his
hilt was sure death, yet he also knew that he could not re-
tain it much longer. Bili had actually bent the fine steel
cuff of his right gauntlet and his relentless pressure was
collapsing the high-grade plate more and more, slowly
crushing the wrist beneath. Then, while their bodies gasped
and thrashed and strained, Bili mindspoke him.

"Ahndee, I don't want to kill you or to see you killed on my account. My mother loves you and I once thought you my friend. What's made you so unreasonable in these last months? Simply that I felt constrained to bring Count Djeen to heel? Why, the High Lord himself averred that the old man had asked for just what he got, and many times over, too."

Ahndros answered telephathically. "You expect me to take your unadorned word on that, do you?"

"If my word isn't sufficient, Ahndee, than why not ask Lord Milo? You have farspeak, he told me, and Whitetip will be happy to assist you."

"I doubt the High Lord would receive my transmission, since I left Vawnpolis without his august leave, lord *thoheeks*. And, even if he did, I'm certain he'd lie to back anything you chose to say. It must have been quite a strain to keep up with the demands of both of them—swiving that slut, Aldora-the-Undying-Whore, then being *poheestos* to Milo."

For a moment, Bili's shock at the accusations sent his mind whirling, then he beamed back, albeit sadly. "You are surely mad, Ahndee, mad as *Vahrohnos* Myros, back in Vawnpolis, gibbering in his cell. I had been warned that there was madness in your house, that too much inbreeding had rendered your strain rotten. Drop your sword, man, stop fighting me, and I'll send you back in honor. Mayhap Master Ahlee can help you return to normalcy."

For a few heartbeats longer, Ahndros maintained the struggle, then he went suddenly limp and his sword clattered from his grasp.

Bili slowly regained his feet, then helped his late opponent to stand. But he missed the feral gleam in Ahndros' black eyes. As the *thoheeks* half-turned to speak to his brother, now standing fully armed at the forefront of the circle of watchers, the *vahrohneeskos* drew his heavy dirk and, screaming, lunged at the hated foe.

Komees Hari's powerful thrust entered the temple, spitting Ahndros's head like an apple on a stick. The black eyes bulged out of their sockets, then a torrent of blood gushed from eyes, ears, nostrils and mouth. The body stiffened, then collapsed bonelessly, the head pulling free of the swordblade with a sucking, popping sound.

During the next few days, Bili took each nobleman and officer aside, separately, and swore them to silence. He loved his mothers and meant to make sure that neither ever would know of how dishonorably *Vahrohneeskos* Ahndros Theftehros of Morguhn had died. To that end, he knew that the late Ahndros's servants would have to be permanently silenced, but to slay all five so close to the death of their master might cause comment amongst the Freefighters, so he simply dragooned them to his own service, where he and his striker could keep tabs on them.

Late the next morning, the vanguard came up to an old battleground, obviously the site of an Ahrmehnee victory, since most of the hacked corpses had been stripped, beheaded and sickeningly mutilated. Due to the almost total absence of artifacts, no one could say for certain just who the more than five score dead men had been; Bili and the others could only assume that they had found a part of Pawl Raikuh's still missing squadron.

In addition to the man-made disfigurements, animals had been at the bodies, and at least a week of sun-drenched days in the open had the dead flesh well on the way to putrefaction, despite the freezing nights. Nonetheless, Bili had troopers examine each cadaver in hopes of establishing his assumption. That was how the odd point was found.

The man who found it, under a reeking corpse, brought it to his captain, and the Freefighter officer immediately rode to the center of the clearing, where Bili and a knot of nobles sat their horses amid the stench.

Captain Krawzmyuh had to almost shout to make himself heard above the angry cawings of the crows and ravens, the flapping of the wings of low-flying buzzards anxious to return to their grisly feasting.

"Duke Bili, Trooper Hwehlbehk found this underneath a body, he did. All the years I been a-soldierin', I ain't seen the like. She 'pears too big and long to be no dart point, but nobody's fool enough to forge barbs on the point of a stabbin' spear."

Bili accepted the piece of metal and scrutinized it. It was about as long as his hand, as the captain had said, too long and heavy to have tipped a hand dart. The steel seemed of poor quality and the forging was rough and sloppy, the hammer marks jaggedly positioned on the faces. Down each edge ran a row of curved barbs, and a couple of inches of sourwood shaft still remained in the band-socket, held by an iron pin. He decided that, whatever had been its use, it was a crude, savage weapon.

While the nobles passed it about amongst themselves, Bili thought aloud. "Barring evidence to the contrary, gentlemen, I think we are safe to assume that these poor bastards were of Captain Raikuh's squadron. But that missle point, if such it actually is, gives one to wonder if their nemesis was really the Ahrmehnee. I find myself doubting it for a number of reasons.

"First, though Ahrmehnee are known to take weapons and armor, horses and their equipage from slain foemen, as well as heads, I've yet to hear of any tribe stripping bodies of clothing and boots. Any nonmetallic item—one which cannot be purified by fire—which was worn touching the skin of a dead enemy is taboo to them, since they much fear the spirits of vengeful victims."

"Yet, my lord," mused Airuhn Mahkai of Duhnkin, "they do take heads . . . ?"

"Which they keep in special, spell-locked houses. And their very real fear is one reason they take heads, Lord Airuhn." Bili had, at the first mention of this campaign, put his keen mind to the task of learning all he could of Ahrmehnee and their ways, so he now spoke with some authority. "Their shamans are of the mind that, so long as they are not unduly angered, maleficent spirits can be kept trapped within their skulls, which never leave the spell-house. But were a spirit to see an Ahrmehnee wearing clothing which once had been worn on that spirit's corporeal body, such would be its anger that it could overcome the spells and wreak terrible vengeance on those who took its life.

"But back to the point, gentlemen. We all are by now aware of the excellence of Ahrmehnee metalworking. They have a passionate love of fine artifacts and are masters at fabricating them. If the High Lord can bring them into the Confederation, give them steady and plentiful sources of raw materials, they'll soon be a very wealthy people, without doubt. Therefore, can any of you imagine an Ahrmehnee warrior willingly entering battle against well-armed men with so ill-wrought and clumsy a weapon? I cannot."

"But, Bili," commented *Komees* Hari, "who else could have mustered the force to slay over a hundred men?"

"Perhaps that tribe the High Lord mentioned, the Muhkohee. They must be powerful if the Ahrmehnee fear them."

"But, my lords," said *Vahrohnos* Raj Graiuhm of Makintahsh, absently massaging the thick neck of his destrier, "according to the maps, we're still two days' march within the borders of the Soormehlyuhn Tribe."

Bili nodded. "According to the maps, baron, but recall if you will what I said at our last meeting before inaugurating the raids. These maps, especially the western borders of them, are of questionable accuracy. Too, even if we are still within the lands of the Ahrmehnee, consider, the bulk of their warriors are long leagues to the northeast and we are not the only men who ever took it into their heads to raid the lands of folk we knew to be occupied with another foe.

"No, gentlemen, I think we had best assume that we could see action at any moment from here on. Accordingly, we'll tighten the march order of the column, bringing the trains from the rear to the center. The cats will still scout our projected route and our extended flanks. But now, between them and the column, a stronger vanguard will ride and, where terrain will permit, flank riders, as well.

"Hari, as you're an old hand at warring and, as you have at least minimal farspeak, you'll command the van. Stay in touch with the cats and with me. If any ambush occurs or if you run into a force unexpectedly, don't try playing the hero, just fight a sensible holding action until the main body gets up to you. Understand? Pick such men as you want. You've your choice of the squadron."

Bili stood up in his stirrups and looked about him, then, raising his voice, called, "Taros? Taros Duhnbahr? Where are you, man?"

When young *Komees* Taros came up, his tall sorrel stallion strutting, Bili told him, "You'll command the rearguards, Taros. I'll assign a cat to pace you on each flank, but keep your eyes peeled. None of us want to end up well-minced buzzard bait. Agreed?"

Earlier that morning, away to the northeast, Aldora and

her *kahtahfrahktoee* had trotted through the *nahkhahrah's* village, then eastward, headed for the gap and the Confederation castra beyond. Insisting upon bringing *Vahrohneeskos* Drehkos with her, Aldora joined Milo in the council house, where she was introduced to the *nahkhahrah* and the assembled *dehrehbehee*. While beer was being poured for the formal healths of welcome, the woman mindspoke Milo.

"Do any of these Ahrmehnee mindspeak?"

Silently, he replied, "The *nahkhahrah* does, I'm sure. And the old man has other powers, as well, powers I can't begin to describe. I don't think even he understands them. Why?"

"I've never understood something about myself, Milo, or about Mara and you and that bastard Demetrios, my dear, departed first husband. At what age do the bodies of the undying stop aging? Do you know?"

Milo shrugged, beaming, "It varies, dear. You look to be about twenty-five, while Mara thinks she stopped at twenty-two or -three. In forty years, Demetrios never looked more than late twentyish, while I've always appeared between thirty and forty. Again, why?"

She smiled cryptically. "Do you think . . . would it be possible for someone to age more than you did and be an Undying? Without him even knowing it?"

"What's all this leading up to, Aldora? Damn it, girl, you can be maddening sometimes. But, in answer, yes, I suppose it would be possible. No one, least of all me, knows enough about our kind to give a definitive answer. And as for not knowing, well, you didn't know and neither did Demetrios, not at first."

"Yes, but then I was a child, mentally, emotionally. As for Demetrios, he was . . . well, to be charitable, always somewhat dense. Could an intelligent man live fifty-odd years and not be aware of his differences?"

Milo's glance shot to Drehkos Daiviz, where he sat sipping Ahrmehnee honeybeer and conversing in broken trade-Mehrikan with a *dehrehbeh*.

"Precisely," Aldora mindspoke. Then she opened her mind to Milo.

From the very beginning to the bloody raid, it had seemed that Drehkos was actively seeking death in battle. He had insisted on commanding the van on marches, and there were few charges during which he was not at the very forefront. His former-rebel horsemen died in droves, but death seemed to flee from his grasp like a will-o'-the-wisp. Then had come that dreadful morning when a large force of screaming, bloodthirsty, vengeance-bent Ahrmehnee warriors had taken Aldora's encampment by surprise.

Suddenly, they had just been there. Rawboned men on foot or on shaggy little ponies, armed with spears and darts, axes and nail-studded clubs, metal-shod targes and wide, straight-bladed, double-edged shortswords. From along the entire southern periphery of the camp they came, wave after yelling, screeching wave of them, grasping brands from the smoldering embers of watchfires and whirling them into full, flaming life, before hurling them into tents or horse lines or among knots of sleep-drugged troopers.

In the rain of darts which followed, many a man died before he even knew the camp to be invaded. Aldora, herself, had been sleeping soundly, but Drehkos had obviously been wakeful, for it was he who organized and led the first resistance. Half-clothed, barefoot, with only a helm and his broadsword, he and a scratch force of camp guards and cats, few of the men fully armed and fewer still mounted, had hurled themselves against three thousand shrieking Ahrmehnee.

While trumpets pealed and drums rolled, while frantic orders were roared and terrified horses screamed even more loudly than the wounded, burning men in the blazing tents, Drehkos and his pitiful few did yeoman service against more than twenty times their numbers. Very few of them lived to see the rise of Sacred Sun, an hour later, and most of those were dead of their many and terrible wounds ere Sun set.

But their sacrifice had saved the camp. Aldora's losses had been heavy, all told, but more than a thousand Ahrmehnee had fallen within the encampment, slain or too badly wounded to flee, as had the bulk of the attackers when at last a sizable number of armed and ordered men confronted them.

There had been a few knots of resistance, though, a few suicide groups who had remained behind to slow pursuit. Bareback, Aldora and her bodyguards had set their horses toward one such, only to see Drehkos and a bare score of his survivors make first, bloody contact. In the few seconds it took for the mounted contingent to reach the broil, half the score were down, lying still in death or gasping and kicking away their last moments of life. Of the rest, none was engaged against any less than three Ahrmehnee.

Even as Aldora had raised and whirled her steel, screaming the Clan Linszee warcry, she had seen Drehkos cut down an Ahrmehnee at the very moment another barbarian jammed a wolfspear into the nobleman's back with such force that the knife-sharp blade emerged, dripping, from his chest. Ere the man could free his spear, Aldora had split his skull with her heavy saber.

When the last Ahrmehnee in camp were cut down, the fires were extinguished and losses were being assessed, Aldora had detailed several of her guardsmen to fetch the *vahrohneeskos'* body and prepare it for cremation. By this time, she was informed of her debt to Drehkos and was truly regretful of the cool formality with which she had rebuffed his overtures of friendship, first at Vawnpolis, then during the raiding campaign.

Guard Lieutenant Trehdhwai shortly rode back to her looking as if he had been clubbed. "My . . . lady, please . . . my lady, you must come and see. He . . . Lord Drehkos is not dead. He—"

"Damnit, Hehrbuht, of course he's dead!" she had snapped peevishly. "Sun and Wind, man, I *saw* one of the swine jam a spear completely through him, back to front. That was over an hour ago. Even if he was not killed at that moment, he's long since bled to death."

But she had gone with the officer.

Drehkos Daiviz of Morguhn was sitting, leaning weakly against a pile of stiffening corpses, his shirtfront stiff and tacky with drying gore. As she dismounted and started wonderingly toward him, one of the ring of guardsmen handed him a canteen from which he drank greedily.

Closing her memory, Aldora recommenced mindspeak. "Milo, I still have that spear. It's got a ten-inch blade, honed as sharp as a sword on both edges. Though they're fading fast, you can still see the two scars on Drehkos' body, one on his back, just under the right shoulderblade, and one on his chest, bisecting his right nipple.

"When I asked him what had happened, he seemed as

stunned as any of us, but quite candidly said that he had fallen face downward and that the fall had pushed the blade back into his body. He just lay there for a while, expecting to die shortly. But he didn't. So, finally, because it was so agonizing, he managed to reach behind him and pull the spear the rest of the way out of him. By the time my guards got to him, he'd stopped bleeding, though the wounds still were gaping when I arrived."

"Who, besides you and them—and him, of course—know of this, Aldora?"

"No one, Milo. I've learned at least that much from you in two hundred years or so."

Milo nodded. "Keep it that way until we're down at the castra. Yes, dear, you're learning. It was most wise to keep him by you . . . whatever it develops he is."

"Bili," Hari mindspoke back from the van, "Whitetip just told me he's found a horse wandering. There's a woman on it, an armored woman, wounded and unconscious. He wants to know if he should lead the horse here or wait for us to come up to him."

"Wait, Hari," Bili replied; then, on farspeak-level, "Catbrother, do you think the female two-leg will fall off the horse if you try to bring her to us?"

"Her kak is like yours, Chief Bili," answered the prairiecat promptly. "She will not fall."

"Then lead the horse to our brother, Hari, catbrother. I will join you there." Then, to Hari, "Watch for Whitetip, he's bringing his find to you. I'll be there as quickly as Mahvros can bear me."

When the black stallion pounded up to the van, Hari and some of his men had removed the rider from her spent, lathered, shuddering horse and laid her out on a cloak. Another cloak had been folded and placed under her head, from which they had removed the dented helm. Using a piece of rag dipped in a waterbag, the old *komees* was gently sponging away the dirt and sweat and blood from her pasty-white face.

Bili had been a warrior for all his adult life and had seen his share of wounds, fatal and otherwise. He shook his head as he strode toward her, thinking that she would not live much longer and that it was a shame, for her features were regular and fair to look upon and her tresses, those not befouled with blood and dirt, were the ruddy black of his stallion's mane, though far finer in texture.

"Isn't she lovely, my lord?" said the husky, red-haired nobleman who strode beside the young *thoheeks*.

Bili didn't answer, for they had reached the wounded woman's side. "Has she said anything, Hari?"

Shaking his head, the old man stood up jerkily, his joints popping and creaking protest. "There's damned little life left in her. She can't even swallow. I tried to give her some brandy and it just ran out of her throat through that wound under her chin. Even if she were conscious, lad, I don't think she'd be able to speak. I tried a scan of her mind, too, but . . ." He shrugged his shoulders and turned up his palms.

Sinking down beside the dying woman, Bili raised one of her eyelids, then straightened and slapped her wan cheeks, hard. His thick, horny hand, hardened by axehaft and swordhilt, with the strength of his brawny arm behind it, cracked cruelly against the chill flesh, right cheek and left, back and palm, in a blur of motion.

Komees Hari was aghast. He stepped forward. "Now, damnit, Bili . . . Sun and Wind, man, what are you doing? You've no call to so abuse her!" he remonstrated, heatedly.

But Bili had stopped. The sooty-lashed eyelids had fluttered ever so faintly and the colorless lips trembled, then passed a croaking moan. After a moment, the lids opened to disclose bloodshot eyes, already beginning to glaze. Roughly, Bili grasped the small head, raised it, and stared hard into those sloe-black pupils.

Chapter IX

"Who are you girl?" he hurriedly mindspoke, sensing that life was almost sped. "Are you of the Moon Maidens? Who wounded you? How far ahead of this place are your sisters?"

Slowly, wonderingly, "But you're a lowlander. How can you speak Ahrmehnee? Please . . . my throat hurts . . . hurts so terribly. And I'm so cold. But, no, Moon Maidens must be strong, must serve Our Lady with stoicism."

Bluntly, "You're dying, sister, you'll not suffer much longer."

A sigh brought dark-pink froth bubbling from her lips and the hole in her throat. Her mind said, "Yes, dying. Soon be one with . . . Lady."

"Who slew you, sister? Was it Muhkohee?"

"Muhkohee, yes, thousands . . . never heard of so many together. Must reach *nahkhahrah*, tell Ahrmehnee, raise all warriors in *stahn*. *Brahbehrnuh* says . . ."

And she was gone.

"Catbrother?" Bili silently called the crouching prairiecat. "Take another and backtrack the horse, but cautiously, for those who slew this female still may watch or follow. I am easier to range than is our brother, Hari, so I will ride with him. Go now, and go quickly."

"Whitetip hears his brother-chief." In one fluid movement, the big, tawny-gray feline rose from his crouch and yawned hugely, his wide pink tongue lolling out between the three-inch-long upper fangs which were a characteristic feature of his species. Whirling, he started off at a distance-eating lope, his thick-thewed legs carrying his several hundred pounds easily over the rock-strewn, steep-graded track. The last Bili saw of him was his bobbing, white-tipped tail, sinking below the crest of the hill ahead.

Remounted, the van continued on, but with intervals of

several yards between each four or six riders. They rode fully alert, the nobles—all save Bili and Hari—with beavers raised and visors lowered and locked. Bili rode with his huge double-bitted axe resting across his flaring pommel, the others with swords bared and targes strapped onto left arms. The archers—every fourth trooper—had all strung their short, powerful hornbows and nocked the steel-shod arrows, gripping two or three more shafts in the fingers of the bowhand, their sabers rattling loose in their cases.

A quarter mile behind, but closing, the main column came; led by Djaik Morguhn and equally ready for battle. Obedient to his older brother's mindspoken command, the deputy quickened the pace until he was within sight of the tail of the van, then slowed to maintain that interval.

One mile they traversed, two, and still the track climbed. Higher, and the footing became treacherous, loose stones atop crumbling rock, all interspersed with had been covered in the Time of the Gods. At one place, shards of that black pebbly substance with which all roads had been covered in the Time of the Gods. At one place, they rode between a double row of ancient columns, cracked and deeply weathered, with rust stains showing through the moss.

Soon after that eerie passage, the footing became firmer and the ascent began to ease, still climbing, but at a more gradual rate. Then the way became level and, around the shoulder of a precipitous hill, they spied a long, wide plateau, beyond which rose another range of dark-green mountains. At that point, Bili halted the column, wary of proceeding into the unknown without foreknowledge of what dangers might lurk there. The word was passed back by mindspeak for the men of the units to dismount but to remain in ranks within easy reach of their mounts.

While awaiting word from the scouting cats, Bili took young Ehrubuhn Duhnkin of Rahbuhtz—the red-haired youngster having ridden all the way from the western marches of the southernmost reaches of the Confederation to join in putting down the rebellion with the *Thoheeks* Duhnkin, his cousin much-removed—and a handful of Freefighter troopers to climb the flanking hill, from the crest of which they could scrutinize the ground ahead.

The menace struck Bili's perceptions full force, wave after irresistible wave, crashing upon him, nearly suffocating him. Yet there was nothing his keen eyes could discern, save the black specks that could only be buzzards, wheeling and dipping over some something about a mile distant, toward the center of the lifeless-looking expanse.

The length of the plateau, which was nowhere indicated on Bili's maps, was, he estimated, at least ten or twelve miles, and the width would probably average half that. Not truly level, it seemed to slope to the southwest, its face furrowed and so deeply eroded that in places it resembled a giant's washboard. Of the stones and boulders which poked through the brush and laurel thickets and sere grass, those close enough for Bili to see well looked unnatural, looked to be weathered but once-worked stone rather than native rocks.

Down to his left, to the south of his present position, several columns of smoke climbed into the sky, though he could not spy either the fires or their makers due to the jagged ridges which lay between. Taking the chance that that was the place from which the dead woman had ridden, he let his open mind range out, questing, in search of the familiar mindpatterns of Whitetip.

"Brother-chief," came the cat's powerful mindspeak, "we just passed through a village. No two-legs live in it. All are dead and headless, even the cubs. It now is impossible to follow the track of the female's horse. Too many horses have passed this way."

Remembering the thick profusion of pony tracks at and around the site of the ambush and battle, Bili asked, "Cat-brother, big hooves or small? Heavy horses or light?"

After a moment the cat replied. "Both, brother-chief, but most of the small were printed over the large. Brother-chief, noise of fighting comes from the place beyond the next hill."

"Then go to the hilltop and tell me what you see," Bili commanded.

Glancing quickly back over the close ground he had earlier scanned, his eyes fixed upon the remembered formation of squarish, mossy rocks and huge-boled old trees which formed a natural fortification atop a small rise and looked about the right size to hold the packtrain.

"Hari," he mindcalled.

"Aye, Bili," came the answer.

"From what Whitetip has seen, we may be fighting soon, and I don't fancy mounting a charge—if we come to that—trailing our trains."

"We can't leave them here, Bili," Hari remonstrated. "This gap could be made a deathtrap, and that right easily, too."

"Yes, you're right, old friend, it's even more evident from here. But about a hundred yards out on the plateau there's a ring of rocks and trees on top of a little hill. I think it's big enough to hold the trains, as well as a couple of troops to defend them. If we—"

"Brother-chief," beamed Whitetip. "Just below me is a big fight." Then he opened his mind so that Bili might see through his eyes.

There was no color, of course, to the battle Bili was witnessing, only varying shades of gray. Against the bare face of a low cliff were drawn up lines of figures who looked, from their armor and equipment, to be women like the one they had found down the trail. There were at least two hundred of them and, with them, were possibly half a thousand Ahrmehnee-looking warriors. The ground before the defensive line—for such it obviously was—lay thickly cobbled with bodies of men and carcasses of horses or ponies. Some of the bodies wore armor but most of them were shaggy and bearded and were covered by nothing more substantial than tattered rags or the skins of animals.

Nor was the source of these bodies difficult to ascertain. Hundreds might lie dead or dying before the hard-pressed women and Ahrmehnee, but thousands—at least two thousand, possibly as many as three—milled about just out of dart range of the line. With Whitetip's keen nose, Bili was aware of the overpowering, nauseous stench of that mob.

He had never seen the like of this horde—hardly any wore helms and their greasy hair hung well below their shoulders, the matted beards of most covered their chests, few looked at all well fed and the majority seemed only bone and sinew and tight-stretched skin; skin long unwashed and scabrous.

Almost all seemed to be big, tall men, their skinny shanks depending amid the thick winter coats of their ill-tended ponies and their largish feet—generally bare, even in this bitter weather—almost dragging the ground. It was obvious that the well-armed men and women would have had little to fear in an open contest with the ruffianish throng had there not been so many of them, for their armament was mostly pitiful—here and there was a sword or an axe or a real lance, but the bulk were furnished only with crude-looking wickerwork targes and a few darts or a stabbing spear or a thick club.

They were formed into no recognizable formations, simply swirling in an aimless manner about several figures looking exactly like themselves, but mounted on full-size horses and fractionally better clad and armed. The cat's ears could register the incessant babble welling up from them. Bili thought that it sounded somewhat similar to some dialects of Mehrikan, but with a whining, twangy quality the like of which he had never before heard. He decided it was as unlovely a language as its speakers.

Then, cantering from out a small patch of bushy evergreens, came another party of the strange barbarians. At the distance, the Northorse at their van looked like a big gray rat leading a herd of mice. Bili was frankly amazed to see a Northorse here in this nameless wilderness, for they were rare enough in more settled lands. The outsize creatures were bred somewhere far to the north of any known lands. The breeders were most astute in maintaining their monopoly of the fabulous and fabulously expensive animals, for they sold but few and then only geldings. In size, they ran from about nineteen hands to as much as twenty-two, and most people saw them only bearing the commodious panniers of traders or in pairs, drawing the huge wains of itinerant merchants.

Northorses were mostly too even-tempered and docile to make good warhorses; nonetheless, some of the wealthier personages of the Middle Kingdoms kept one in their stables. Bili could recall how the king of Harzburk, massive as he was, had looked like a mere toddler astride a destrier on the bay Northorse he used for parades. But not so the man—if man born of woman he truly was—who bestrode yonder Northorse.

Bili knew that he had never seen a man so huge, and he doubted if anyone else, even the High Lord, had. Standing on his gigantic feet, the barbarian would surely overtop *nine feet*! Some unidentifiable fur enwrapped his barrel-thick torso, concealing any armor the giant might be wearing, but head and face were covered by a shiny helm, beaver and visor. Over his left shoulder, its hilt lost in his gargantuan left hand, rested the wide, heavy-looking blade of a broadsword, and that blade was no less than six feet long. Across his back was slung a sheaf of what, to him, were probably hand darts, but Bili thought he had seen shorter boarspears.

The moment he came within sight of his motley throng, thousands of throats commenced a deep roar of "*BUHBUH! BUHBUH! BUHBUH!*"

The treetrunk-thick arm raised and flourished the immense sword, then pointed it at the few hundred armored figures at the base of the cliff. But Bili had seen enough. He withdrew from Whitetip's mind, first admonishing him, "Cat-brother, stay hidden where you are until we arrive. One or two cats, no matter how strong and valiant, could accomplish little against so many two-legs."

Bili left only a half-troop with the trains. If the battle should go against him, whatever remnants of the squadron were left could withdraw to the position and try either to hold the strongpoint or, if it seemed advisable, flee back the way they had come onto the plateau. Meanwhile, he wanted every sword he could get behind him when he attacked those thousands of barbarians.

When he had described what Whitetip's eyes had seen to Hari and certain of the others, the old nobleman had protested, "Bili, lad, I like a fight as much as any other, but . . . *three thousand men*, and us less than a thousand? And don't forget the High Lord's mission, his instructions."

"I'm not forgetting either, Hari," Bili replied grimly. "But aside from the fact that those folk, whoever they be, probably owe me bloodprice, for the butchery of Raikuh's squadron, we have no choice. Our path lies straight across this plateau, and I don't want the likes of them snuffing out our trail or barring our return. Do you?"

"Well, no, Bili, but—"

"I'd rather fight them now, on my terms, than later, on theirs and at a place of their choosing. Too, if the Ahrmehnee are now our allies, we can't just ride on and let them be massacred by a pack of human wolves, can we?"

Behind several lines of pickets, with outriders thrown

well out to van and flanks, the squadron made a rapid advance despite the difficult, uneven terrain. Along with the background rumble of thudding hooves, armor clanked and leather creaked, equipment thunked and metal-fittings jangled, but Bili knew that the noises were unimportant, for none would hear them above the din of battle even if distance and the folds of ground failed to muffle them.

A quarter-hour brought the van to the outskirts of the village mentioned by the cat. And all was just as Whitetip had described it. It had been a small place, only a bare dozen small cabins of dry-stone construction, thick, windowless walls and thatched roofs. But those roofs had all been burnt off and smoke still curled up from within those walls, along with the stink of charring flesh. All among the ruined houses lay stripped, hacked, headless bodies of both sexes and of sizes varying from infant to adult.

All the men of Bili's squadron were soldiers who had witnessed the horrors of war at first hand. Most of them were professionals and had devoted the larger portion of their lives to traveling from one bloody battle to the next. Even the southern nobles, those who had never been professionals, had lived through the incredible carnage of the siege of Vawnpolis or had ridden with Bili to put down the rebellion in Morguhn. But the evidences of unhallowed atrocity which lay athwart the path of the squadron had more than a few men frantically unlocking visors and fighting down beavers that the interiors of their helms might not be befouled with the spewed contents of their stomachs.

Just below the crest of the hill, Bili halted his command and, along with Hari and Taros, who would captain the right and left wings, bellied into the thicket which concealed Whitetip and the other cat.

The scene Bili now saw with his own eyes was very similar to that seen earlier through the eyes of the huge cat. There seemed to be slightly fewer of the shaggy men milling about their gigantic leader and a somewhat denser carpet of bodies between the horde and the cliff. But there were definitely fewer of the Ahrmehnee, far fewer. Their lines were considerably contracted in length and the depth of their formation was much reduced. But they stood firm in the face of the death which must surely overtake most of them when next they were attacked. Men and women leaned, panting, on their well-used weapons in grim silence. Behind their lines lay their wounded or dead, and within cave mouths in the base of the cliffside Bili thought he could discern the heads of horses.

The top of the cliff was a continuation of the crest of the hill on which the men and cats lay, though the slope before them was much more gradual than it became as it curved around closer to the sheer precipice. A charge down this slope would take the attackers of the Ahrmehnee on the right flank and, were the line strung long enough, at the right rear, as well. Squinting in concentration, the young *thoheeks* considered every angle of the projected charge, weighed up every misfortune which might befall and racked his brain to settle upon an alternate plan of action to counter each. At length, he slid his armored body back down from the thicketed crest, signaling the two nobles to follow but mindspeaking the cats to remain, bidding them let him know when the barbarians seemed on the verge of a fresh assault.

Back at the squadron, he summoned the nobles and Freefighter officers and first outlined his strategy, then issued succinct commands.

All was in readiness before the undisciplined rabble, screaming and howling like wild beasts, started to cover the distance separating them from the battered little band opposing them. Bili and the others did not need Whitetip's mindspeak to tell them, for the thud-thudding of the thousands of pony hooves was clearly audible. A ripple of movement went all through the ranks of armored horsemen as visors were snapped shut and locked onto beavers. Then Bili kneed Mahvros forward and, behind him, his squadron advanced uphill, toward the crest.

On the floor of the wide defile, the shaggy men on their shaggy ponies roiled ahead, presenting a jagged front as faster ponies surged uncontrolled and slower ones lagged. Few darts flew between the two groups, for nearly all had been expended during the earlier engagements. All at once, though, furry figures commenced to drop their crude weapons while emitting shrieks of agony, to reel from off their mounts and be trampled under the heedless hooves of the riders who followed. The Ahrmehnee seemed as shocked as the barbarians at the drizzle of slender shafts, seemingly from the empty sky.

The brow of the cliff hid from the Ahrmehnee the stag-
gered line of bowmasters, but the barbarians could see
them, and increasing dozens of them felt the deadly bite of
the arrows. But the advance neither slowed nor faltered.
As the range decreased, more shafts homed into flesh and
the dozens became scores. Wounded ponies screamed and
reared or fell with their riders, to die messily as the thousands galloped over them.

At the crest, Bili halted for half a heartbeat, taking in
the panorama spread below. The giant was now among the
rearmost of the horde—Northorses being bred for strength
and endurance rather than speed, even the comparatively
tiny ponies were far faster at the gallop. The big gray lum-
bered along, the monster who bestrode him waving his impossibly long blade, his huge maw gaping, his roars lost in
the general din.

"Sun and Wind!" swore *Komees* Hari. "Yon's not a
man, it's surely a monster!"

Taking a fresh grip on the steel haft of his massive axe,
Bili mindspoke his stallion. "Now, brother-mine, now we
fight."

With Bili and a knot of heavily armed nobles at the
center, the squadron crested the hill and swept down the
slope at a jarring gallop. Naturally, a few horses fell, but
only a few. As they reached level ground, Hari's wing, the
left, extended to take aim at the rear of the unruly mob of
pony riders. And, all the while, the bowmasters sustained
their rain of death upon the forefront of the host.

Bili unconsciously tightened his leg muscles, firming his
seat and crowding his buttocks against the cantle, while
crouching over the thundering black's neck and extending
his axe at the end of his strong right arm, the sharp spike
at the business end of that shaft glinting evilly in the pale
rays of sun.

And then they struck!

The big, heavy, war-trained horses sent ponies tumbling
like ninepins, and the well-armed, steel-sheathed nobles
and Freefighters wreaked fearful carnage among the unarmored and all but defenseless barbarians. The Ahrmehnee
could only stand speechless with the wonder of this elev-
enth-hour deliverance from what must surely have been
their last battle.

A red-bearded headhunter heeled his pony at Bili and

jabbed furiously with his spear, but the soft iron point bent against the Pitzburk plate and Bili's axe severed the speararm, cleanly, at the shoulder. Screaming a shrill challenge, Mahvros reared above a pony and rider and came down upon them, steel-shod hooves flailing; gelatinous globs of brain spurted from the man's shattered skull and the pony collapsed under the weight, whereupon the killer stallion stove in its ribs.

It was a battle wherein living men were a-horse. Those not mounted—noble, Freefighter or barbarian—were speedily pounded into the blood-soaked ground. The shaggy men fell like ripe grain, most of their weapons almost useless when pitted against fine, modern plate and only slightly more effective when employed against the scalemail hauberks of the Freefighters. To counter blows and thrusts of broadsword and saber, axe and lance, the primitive wickerwork targes offered no more protection than did the hides and ragged homespun clothing.

But, though the shaggy men died in droves, it seemed to Bili that there were always more and yet more appearing before him, behind him, to each side of him, jabbing spears and beating on his plate with light axes, with crude blades and wooden clubs. He felt that he had been fighting, slaying, swinging his ever-heavier axe for centuries. But, abruptly, he was alone, with none before him or to either side. At a flicker of movement to his right, he twisted in his sweaty saddle, whirling up his gore-clotted axe.

But it was only a limping, riderless pony, hobbling as fast as he could go from that murderous engagement, eyes rolling wildly and nostrils dilated. Bili slowly lowered his axe and relaxed for a brief moment, slumped in his saddle, drawing long, gasping, shuddery breaths. Beneath his three-quarter armor and the padded, leather gambeson, he seemed to be only one long, dull ache, with here and there sharper pains which told of strained muscles, while his head throbbed its resentment of so many clanging blows on the protecting helm. Running his parched tongue over his lips, he could taste the sweat bathing his face as well as the salty blood trickling from his nose, but he seemed to be unwounded.

Several more stampeding ponies passed by while he sat and one or two troop horses, the last with a Freefighter reeling in the kak, rhythmically spurting bright blood from a left arm that ended just above the elbow. Exerting every ounce of willpower, Bili straightened his body and reined Mahvros about, bringing up his ton-heavy axe to where he could rest its shaft across his pommel.

Fifty yards distant, the battle still surged and raged. He had ridden completely through the widest, densest part of the howling horde, a testament to Mahvros' weight and bulk and ferocity as much as to his rider's fighting skills. So close that he could almost touch him stood a panting horse and a panting rider. There was no recognizing who might be within the scarred and dented plate, but Bili knew that mare and nudged Mahvros nearer.

When they sat knee to knee, he leaned close and shouted, "Geros! Sir Geros! Are you hurt, man?" His voice thundered within his closed helm. "Where in hell did you get my Eagle?"

But the other rider sat unmoving, unresponsive. His steel-plated shoulders rose and fell jerkily to his heavy, spasmodic breathing. One gauntleted fist gripped the hilt of his broadsword, its blade red-smeared from point to guard; the other held a hacked and splintery ashwood shaft, from which the tattered and faded Red Eagle of Morguhn banner rippled silkily in the freshening breeze. Sir Geros had borne this banner to glory and lasting fame while serving with Pawl Raikuh's Morguhn Troop of Freefighters, but since his elevation to the ranks of the nobility—after a singular act of valor done during the early days of the siege of Vawnpolis—a common trooper had been chosen standardbearer, the new knight taking his well-earned place among the heavily armed nobles.

Bili tried mindspeak. "Did you piss your breeks, as usual, Sir Geros?"

Contrition boiled up from the knight's soul and beamed out with the reply. "I always do, my lord, always befoul myself in battle."

Bili chuckled good-naturedly and his mirth was silently transmitted as well. "Geros, every manjack in this squadron knows you've got at least a full league of guts. When are you going to stop being ashamed of the piddling fact that your bladder's not as brave as the rest of you, man? None of us give a damn, why should you?"

"But . . . but, my lord, it . . . it's not *manly*."

Bili snorted derision. "Horse turds, Sir Geros! You're acknowledged one of the ten best swordsmen in a dozen duchies and you fight like a scalded treecat, so why worry about a meaningless quirk of yours? No one else is bothered by it."

"There is never a fight, my lord, but that someone mentions my weakness, asks of it or openly lays hand to my saddle or my breeks. Then they all laugh."

Bili extended his bridle hand to firmly grip the knight's shoulder, chiding gently, "Geros, Geros, the laughter is at your evident embarrassment, and it's friendly, well-meant joshing. There are few men in all the host as widely and deeply respected as are you. Everyone knows you're a brave man, Geros."

Geros shook his head, tiredly. "But I'm not really brave, my lord, and *I* know it. I fight for the same reason I strove to master the sword, only to stay alive. And I'm frightened near to death, almost all the time. That's not valor, my lord."

"Not so!" stated Bili firmly. "It's the highest degree of valor, that you recognize and accept your fears and then do your duty despite them. And don't you forget what poor old Pawl Raikuh told you that day before we stormed the salients. Fear, controlled fear, is what keeps a warrior alive in a press. Men who don't know fear seldom outlive their first serious battle.

"Geros, self-doubt is a good thing in many ways; it teaches a man humility. But you can't let yourself be carried too far by such doubts, else they'll unman you.

"But, tell me, how did you chance to be bearing my banner again? Can't keep your hands off it, eh?"

Geros was too exhausted and drained to rise to the joke. "My lord, I was riding at Klifuhd's side through most of that ghastly mess back there and I thought me I had guarded him and the Eagle well. Then just at the near fringes of the horde, a barbarian axeman crowded between us and lopped off poor Klifuhd's forearm. I ran the stinking savage through the body and barely caught the Eagle ere it fell. Then I was in the open here. I don't know what happened to Klifuhd, my lord."

"Well, man, you have it now. How's your throat? Dry as mine, I don't doubt." Feeling behind his saddle, he grunted satisfaction at finding his canteen still in place.

With numbed, twitching fingers, he unlatched his visor and lowered his beaver. Raising the quart bottle to his crusty lips, he filled his mouth once and spat it out, then took several long drafts of the brandy-and-water mixture. The first swallow burned his gullet ferociously, like a red-hot spearblade on an open wound, but those which followed it were as welcome and soothing as warm honey. Taking the bottle down at last, he proffered it to Sir Geros.

"Here, man, wash your mouth and oil that remarkable set of vocal cords. If we're to really clobber these bastards, we must rally the squadron and hit them hard again."

The impetus of that smashing charge had been lost, and the majority of the lowland horsemen were fighting alone or in small groups, rising and falling from sight, almost lost in a shifting sea of multi-toned, shaggy fur. Bili realized that where mere skill at arms and superior armor could not promise victory or even survival against such odds, the superior bulk and weighty force of the troop horses and destriers were his outnumbered squadron's single remaining asset. But to take full advantage of those assets, the horde must again be struck by an ordered, disciplined formation, charging at a gallop. But before he could deliver another crushing charge, he must rally his scattered elements . . . such of them as he could.

Chapter X

And once more, Geros' clear tenor voice pealed like a trumpet above the uproar, while Bili gripped the brass-shod ferrule in both his big hands, raised the banner high above his head and waggled the shaft. For a long, breathless moment, it seemed that none could or would respond to the summons, but a pair of blood-splashed Freefighters hacked their way from out of the near edge of the press, then a half-dozen more appeared behind a destrier-mounted nobleman. Slowly, by dribbles and drops, the squadron's ranks again filled and formed up behind the Red Eagle.

Not all those who had made that first charge returned, of course. Some were just too hard pressed to win free; some would never return. Bili took a position a good two hundred yards off the left flank of the milling mob, the absolute minimum distance cavalry needed to achieve the proper impetus in a charge. He had just gotten the under-strength troops into squadron-front—shortened squadron-front—when the beat of hundreds of hooves sounded from somewhere within the narrow defile at his own left flank. The veteran troopers were already preparing to wheel in order to meet the self-announced menace, when the riders swept from the mouth of that precipitous gap. In the lead rode Ehrbuhn Duhnkin—recognizable because of his clean, unmarred armor—followed by the bowmasters he had commanded to such good effect. But now bows were all unstrung and cased, sabers were out and flashing in the sunlight.

While the Freefighters took their accustomed places in the shrunken ranks, Ehrbuhn rode up to the young *thoheeks*, mindspeaking, "We had to miss first blood, Lord Bili, but I mean to be in at the kill. So do some others, incidentally. They it was who showed us the way here. In

114

all courtesy, my lord, I think we should not begin the dance until the ladies arrive."

With the Maidens riding in a place of honor on the exposed right flank and the grim-faced *brahbehrnuh* just behind Bili in the knot of heavily armed nobles at the center, the reformed and reinforced squadron struck the confused and reeling barbarians almost as hard as they had the first time. And human flesh could take no more. The savages broke, scattered before the big horses and armored warriors and streamed down the narrow vale in full flight.

Some escaped, but not many. The destriers and troop horses were tired, true, but so too were the ponies. Superior breeding and carefully nurtured top condition told in the end, at a cost of the ultimate price to most of the barbarians. The shaggy men were pursued to the very end of the long plateau, ridden down and slain. Then Bili forced a halt and rallied his force before commencing the slow, weary march back to the battlefield below the cliff.

Bili trudged beside Mahvros at the head of the exhausted squadron, having allowed none save the wounded to remain mounted. The black stallion was spent; he seemed barely able to place one hoof before the other and his proud head hung low, his shiny hide now befouled with dried lather and old sweat, with horse blood and man blood and dust. Nor were the other horses of the battered squadron in better shape; many were, in fact, in worse.

The *brahbehrnuh* helped a reeling Freefighter onto the back of her relatively fresh charger and then strode up to pace beside Bili. After a moment, she addressed him in accented but passable trade Mehrikan.

"What is the polite form of address for my lord?" Still plodding, Bili turned his shaven head and looked into her bloodshot eyes, smiling tiredly.

"The Ehleenee say '*thoheeks*,' my Freefighters say 'duke' and my friends call me simply 'Bili.' You are free to use whichever comes easiest to your lips, my lady."

With a brusque nod of her helmeted head, she asked bluntly, "You and your folk are the born enemies of the Ahrmehnee and, indirectly, of me and my sisters. So then why do you fight and bleed and die for us? Was there not enough loot in the vales for both you and the cursed Muhkohee? Think you that even this will earn you

Ahrmehnee forgiveness for your many and heinous crimes, Dookh Bili?"

A woman of spirit, thought Bili—no polite, meaningless words for her; she spits it right out and be damned to you if you don't like it. "Because, my lady, me and mine no longer are the enemies of the Ahrmehnee. Even now does their great chief treat with our High Lord, and, soon, all these Ahrmehnee mountains and vales will be one with our mighty Federation of Peoples, your folk too, probably."

"Never!" she spat. "Since the Time of the Earth-Gods have the Moon Maidens been sensibly ruled by women. Never will we submit to the utter debasement of the rule of mere men!"

Then did Bili Morguhn show a spark of that genius which was to win him a place high in the councils of his homeland. "But, my lady, did you not know?"

"Know what, lowlander?"

"Why this, my lady—the true rulers of the Confederation *are* women, the Undying High Ladies, Mara Morai and Aldora Linszee Treeah-Pohtohmas Pahpahs."

Her jaw dropped open in wonderment, but she quickly recovered. "Then what of your infamous Undying Devil, this Milo?"

"Lord Milo commands the Confederation armies, especially in the field on campaign," Bili answered glibly. "You see, our armies are all of men."

Her high brow wrinkled. "But, Dookh Bili, how can these High Ladies trust this Milo to not treacherously bring the armies against them, slay them and usurp their rightful place? The men of my own folk foolishly tried such many times over the centuries until, finally, we forbade mere men to carry weapons or know their use." She smiled grimly. "That was in the time of my mother's mother's grandmother, and the Wise Women have ruled, unquestioned and unopposed, since."

Bili shook his head. "Such harsh measures are generally unneeded in the lands of the Confederation, my lady. For one thing, the Undying High Ladies cannot be slain with weapons, but, more importantly, the High Lord would never do aught which might harm the Confederation. Moreover, he loves the Lady Mara and has great respect for the Lady Aldora. Thus has it been for six generations and more."

They walked on in silence for a quarter-hour. At last, the *brahbehrnuh* announced, "When and where and how can I meet with one of these High Ladies, Doohk Bili? With our hold destroyed, we are cast adrift in a hostile world, with naught save the little we bear and wear. But I must be certain that my sisters and I—who are the last, pitiful remnant of our race, now—will receive land in return for our allegiances and service to your Lady rulers and that we will be allowed to practice our ancient rites and customs unmolested. These things must your Ladies avow to us who serve the Supreme Lady."

Bili mused, trying to guess just what to say to this strange, handsome young woman, but, abruptly, the conversation became unimportant.

Many leagues to the north and west, in what had been the Hold of the Maidens, a defective timing device at last fulfilled its long-overdue function. A small charge exploded, hurling a barrel-size charge over the lip of the smoking fissure which was known as the Sacred Hoofprint. Far it fell, deeper and deeper into the very bowels of the uneasy mountain, into hotter and hotter regions, falling within bare seconds from degrees of hundreds into degrees of thousands. And, still falling free, its metal casing began to melt, dripping away, and its insulation burst into brief flame and then the immense charge exploded, its sound unheard by living ear.

A feeling of unbearable unease suddenly gripped Bili. His every nerve ending seemed to be screaming, *"DANGER! DANGER! DANGER!"*

Tired as they were, all the horses were uneasy, too, snorting and nodding, their nostrils dilated and eyes rolling, dancing with nervousness. As for Mahvros, the big black suddenly half-reared and almost bolted when three deer broke cover, dashing out of a dark copse to rocket downslope and over the edge of the plateau. Hard on their heels came a living carpet of small, scuttling beasts and, up ahead, a pair of mountain wolves and a tree cat loped along in the same direction, almost side by side.

Recalling that the High Lord had said prairiecats were but a mutation of tree cats and that many specimens of the latter could mindspeak, Bili attempted to range the fleeing feline but encountered only a jumble of inchoate terror.

Bili allowed his instinct to command him. "*MOUNT!*" he roared to those behind. "Mount and form column!" Following his own order, his weariness clean forgotten, he flung himself astride Mahvros, slapping his gambeson hood and helm back in place.

He had but barely forked his steed when the very earth shuddered strongly. Horses screamed; so, too, did some of the humans. The *brahbehrnuh* stumbled against the side of the dancing stallion, frantically grasping Bili's stirrup leather for the support her feet could not find on the rippling ground. With no time or care for niceties, Bili grabbed the woman's swordbelt and, lifting her effortlessly, placed her belly-down on his crupper.

Komees Hari came alongside, his big gray tight-reined. "It can only be an earthquake, Bili. I thought there was something odd about this damned plateau. We've got to get off it."

"*THAT WAY!*" Bili shouted, pointing to where the animals had disappeared, a hundred yards to his right. Mahvros was too submerged in terror to respond to mindspeak, so Bili reined him over. His booted heels beat a tattoo on the destrier's barrel and evoked a willing response; exhaustion forgotten, the big black raced flat out in the track of the fleeing game beasts.

The column followed, while trees crashed around them and boulders shifted, slid and tumbled. After their lord they went, heedlessly putting their mounts at the impossibly narrow descent down the precipitous face of the plateau. Had the plateau been higher, none would have survived. Since it was much lower than in the northern reaches, all save the very tail of the line were galloping hard toward the south when, with a horrible, grinding roar, the entire rocky face dissolved and slid down upon itself.

Not until they were a bird-flight mile from what had been the foot of the plateau did Bili bring his command to a walk, then a halt on the brushy slope of a long, serpentine ridge. Not even there was the earth completely still, but the occasional tremors were quickly forgotten, erased from their minds by the terrible wonder on the northern horizon.

So huge that it looked close enough to touch, a boiling cloud of dense, multicolored smoke loomed, shot through with flame for all its immense and increasing height. Then with a clap of such magnitude that horses screamed and reared, while men and women slapped hands to abused ears and rolled on the heaving hillside in agony, some force shredded the cloud, leaving only tumbling, smoking black shapes of irregular conformation, rising, rising and whirling, then falling swiftly. And where, within sight, those shapes grounded, smoke and leaping flames burst up. One of the shapes fell, bouncing heavily, in the tiny vale betwixt the ridge and the hill beyond. It came finally to rest in an almost-dry streambed and, when the last tendrils of stream had died, Bili and the others could clearly see that it was simply a boulder. But what a boulder! A boulder big enough for two destriers to have stood upon, uncrowded.

And upon its broad face, certain cryptic carvings were plainly visible. At sight of them, the *brahbehrnuh* uttered a single, piercing shriek. Then her eyes rolled back in their sockets and she collapsed, bonelessly, at Bili's feet.

Regardless of the gruesome task he had so recently completed, Master Ahlee's garments and person were spotless when he came to render his report to *Strahteegos* Vaskos Daiviz of Morguhn. He had commanded the medical contingent of the High Lord's force and, as soon as it had become apparent that the battle with the Ahrmehnee was over, he had returned to Vawnpolis, where many folk were still suffering from the aftereffects of the long, hard siege.

Vaskos had been more than glad to have the erudite, skillful Zahrtohgahn physician, and not only because of the good his ministrations could do the Vawnpolisee who were the responsibility of the conscientious officer. For these two men had been friends for nearly a year, since the brown-skinned master had successfully treated the grievous wounds Vaskos had suffered when he had fought his way out of rebel-held Horse Hall, in the first days of the short-lived rebellion in Morguhn. That friendship had ripened during the protracted siege of Vawnpolis as they met whenever their various duties had permitted to share an ewer of wine and engage in the Game of Battles, at which both excelled, or exchange anecdotes of travels and combat.

Utterly stymied by the seemingly insoluble problem of the frequent murders, all his own efforts and those of his staff having failed, Vaskos had finally discussed the matter with Ahlee. And that was why, this day, the master had just completed the autopsy of the seventh young woman murdered in as many weeks.

Shoving aside a mound of papers and flexing his ink-stained fingers, Vaskos pushed himself back from his desk and, smiling, waved the master toward a chair.

"You are overtired, Vaskos," chided Ahlee gently. "Of what use will you be to the High Lord if you break your health? Your staff is both large and competent, yet you put them in armor on city patrols and then try to do their work yourself. Promise an old man that you will promptly mend your ways."

Vaskos sighed, frowning. "Master, I have armed all the ex-rebels I dare to. Too, I have begged all the troops I can reasonably expect from *Strahteegos* Demosthenos, out at the base camp. My staff noncoms were all the men I had left, with the exceptions of Danos' crew, and those poor bastards have been standing watch on watch for months. I couldn't bring myself to ask more of them . . . or him, either, much as I hate him. I doubt me if the Ehleen god could fabricate a worse punishment than he is living in."

Ahlee shook his scarred, brown head—hairless, like the rest of his body, for reasons of cleanliness. "Vaskos, my friend, my order is dedicated to the saving of life in accordance with Ahláh's Holy Will. I have served that order for the larger part of my life. Consequently, it pains me to suggest that you have the *Vahrohnos* Myros Deskati . . . ahhh, put out of his misery. The man is, in my humble opinion, incurable and is just too dangerous to maintain longer in the existing manner. He has a record of having already slain one member of Captain Danos' detachment, and that man he attacked last week will be crippled for the rest of his days."

"I'd dearly love to do it," grunted Vaskos. "Personally. Were it my decision to make, I'd hump myself down to that level and put my sword in the bastard in an eyetwinkling. But he be the prisoner of my overlord . . . well, my father's overlord, anyhow. And I don't think *Thoheeks* Bili would be too happy were he denied hearing Myros' death screams, considering all the merry hob the whoreson raised in Morguhn."

At the last word, Vaskos rose and stumped over to a heavy tapestry. Pulling it back, he took from the arrowslit window it covered a jar of wine, now cooled by the frigid outdoor temperature. Setting the jar on his desk, he crossed to the hearth and poked up the fire, then returned to his seat and poured two mugs full.

When Ahlee had sipped, the *strahteegos* said, "Well, did you learn anything new from this latest victim, master?"

The white-robed physician shrugged. "In point of fact, Vaskos, no. Her injuries were almost identical to those of all the other poor women; I can attest that all were even mutilated with the same instruments."

"And what of the monster who wielded them, master? Any inkling of who we're looking for?"

"As I said often before, Vaskos, you are looking for a madman who, with all the cunning of his madness, has thus far eluded you. Could you but take me to the place wherein he does his savageries, I could perhaps tell you more concerning him. But then, if you knew where he takes his victims, you would need nothing save patience in order to apprehend him."

"If! If! If!" Vaskos' bloodshot eyes blazed his ill-controlled wrath and he slammed his callused palm onto the desktop. "Meanwhile, this rebel bastard of a woman killer goes his merry, bloody way making fools out of me and the entire Confederation garrison. Sun blast the swine! *Why* can't we catch him?"

They very nearly had on two occasions, and Captain Danos still became pale and weak-kneed whenever he thought of how narrow had been his two escapes. And what made the terrible chances he was daring so meaningless was the awful fact that he no longer even enjoyed himself. Had not since the devil-spawn *vahrohnos* had demonstrated that, though he might be Danos' prisoner, still was he the captain's master.

Always had it been the cries of his victims—the moans, the whimpering pleas for mercy and, especially, the screams of agony—which had aroused Danos' sexual lusts. But now, with the streets above his well-concealed cellar aswarm with armed and alert men, he was afraid to allow any avoidable noise from his victims. And victims were becoming harder and harder to come by. Only his thorough knowledge of Vawnpolis and its secret ways had provided him with the last half-dozen women and with a means of getting them onto that bloodstained cellar floor under the ruined mansion. And he knew with utter certainty that it was but a matter of time—possibly a rather short time—until one of the roving parties chanced upon an arm of that warren of ancient tunnels.

Quite by accident, he had stumbled into the subterranean ways during the siege when an overshot catapult stone had demolished some of the charred timbers and fire-blackened bricks of the once splendid mansion above his chamber of horrors. These were quite unlike the great tunnels under Morguhnpolis, being no more than six feet high and five wide, unpaved and shored up by old, rotting timbers. The main passage ran from east to south on a gradual curve, ending at each extremity against the damp stones of the city walls, and it was unblocked from one end to the other. Such was not true of many of the branch passages. Danos had found that many had collapsed and others seemed so close to collapse that he had feared to enter them.

But that had been before the increasing security within the city and the steady pressure from the satanic *vahrohnos* had so complicated his existence. Now he regularly trod fearfully beneath sagging, wormy timbers and even wriggled through partially blocked passages in search of access to fresh prey. The arm leading to the Citadel, though not paved, was at least walled and shored with granite, probably because of the immense weight of masonry above it. It debouched into a disused subcellar room, only four levels below the prison corridor off which was located the *vahrohnos'* cell, which fact was the sole reason, aside from inordinate amounts of pure luck, that Danos had not long since been apprehended.

Both of his close escapes had occurred when Danos was returning to the Citadel in the early morning. If, as in the old days, he had come back smeared from head to foot with the blood of his night's victim, the jig would have been up. But Danos had begun to take precautions to minimize the possibility of discovery and, having come across a small, spring-fed cistern in the main passage, he always thoroughly cleansed himself, his armor and his clothing after each of his forays.

No, what had most frightened him about the encounters with Citadel guards had been that, on each occasion, he had been carrying back the "delicacies" demanded by the *vahrohnos*. And had the guards ever chosen to examine the two sealed jars, there would have been no possible way that Captain Danos could have explained why one was brimful of fresh blood, while the other contained a whole human liver, still warm.

It had been after that second episode in the lower corridors that he had finally convinced the mad *vahrohnos* that he could no longer take the risk of carrying the "delicacies" into the Citadel.

After an impossibly long moment of glowering at his warder from eyes deep-sunk in his ruined face, Myros of Deskati had smiled, albeit wolfishly. "It is in moments of extreme danger that breeding becomes apparent, and you have no trace of breeding, you lowborn swine. But I had been expecting this funk of yours, soon or late, and I have devised an alternate plan, one which will give you far less to fear . . . well, from the guards, anyway."

Since Vaskos had refused to alter or lessen his long, work-filled hours, Ahlee had done what he felt to be both professional duty and the duty of a friend; he had been helping the harried commander with the paperwork, of nights. Nor was this a difficult undertaking for the Zahrtohguhn, for, combined with a high degree of intelligence and both a written and verbal command of most dialects of Mehrikan, Ahlee had a natural talent for and formal training in mindspeak so that he could resolve any questions by dipping into Vaskos' deliberately unshielded mind.

So it was, on an evening six days after his last autopsy, that a breathless, red-faced sergeant found them both together in Vaskos' bright-lit office a couple of hours after midnight.

The sergeant was not an ex-rebel but rather a grizzled Confederation Regular, and he behaved accordingly despite his agitation—this quite obvious to Ahlee's trained eye. Upon being bidden to enter, he stalked stiffly across the room, his well-oiled armor clanking, his helm cradled

in the crook of his shield arm. At the halt, he wheeled precisely to face the desk and, standing rigid as a post,
slammed fist against breast in formal military salute.

Glancing up from under his bushy salt-and-pepper
brows, Vaskos returned the salute. "Yes, sergeant? You
have a report?"

In a firm, emotionless voice, the noncom replied, "My
lord *strahteegos*, I be Company Sergeant Dahbzuhn of
Number Three Company, Fourteenth Regiment, seconded
to your lordship's command and now serving under Lieutenant Gahloopohlos. The noble lieutenant bids me request
your lordship's presence in the north quarter of the city.
And it please your lordship, immediately."

The lieutenant was tall but slender, his dark hair and olive complexion attesting to his Ehleen antecedents. His
were no rolling, bulging muscles, but he moved with an as-
surance and grace which Ahlee suspected emanated from
considerable wiry strength. The young man was soft-
voiced and respectful to his superior but with no trace of
fawning.

"My lord *strahteegos*, knowing how intense be your in-
terest in these murders, I took the liberty of sending for
you. This may well be a discovery of importance."

The one-eyed man, summoned from a small knot of fellow civilians, completed his tale a few minutes later. "So,
like I a'ready done told the lieutenant, Lord Vaskos, after
I seen the man knock Moynah in the head and put her
over his shoulder, I follered him, 'th out him seeing' me,
o'course; I ain't brave, 'specially as I seen he had a big
dirk.

"I seen him carry her into this here empty house, then I
run back and got these here other fellers together and
while one feller went to look for the p'trol, we got us some
torches and clubs and a few knives and went to save her.
But, when we got to the house, won't nary a sign of either
one of 'em, 'cept just a little bit of blood just inside the
door and a little more on the steps going down to the
basement, was all. Then, 'bout that time, the lieutenant
and the p'trol got here."

With a brusque nod of thanks to the old man, Vaskos
turned on the junior officer. "It comes to my mind that the
killer, if such it was, knew that he was being followed and

ducked into the house until he was certain that the observer had gone. Could that be possible, lieutenant?"

With a typically Ehleenic shrug, Gahloopohlos answered, "Highly possible, lord *strahteegos*. And I considered it, too, especially when my men found no living creature in the house . . . and we searched it from top to bottom. But that was before we chanced across what I wish to now show your lordship."

The cellar was old, obviously much older than the house above, larger, too, walled and floored with dressed stone, like the worn stairs which led down to it. Droplets of blood were at the head of those stairs, a few more were at the bottom, and yet another sprinkling was at a spot near the east wall of the cellar, along with a faded scrap of fine woolen cloth.

"When first I came down here, my lord, this bit of cloth was protruding from between two of the wall stones. I thought it odd and examined the wall more closely. As my lord may know, my father is lord architect of Kehnooryos Atheenahs. My brothers and I often accompanied him in his duties in that and other cities, so I have some small knowledge of things which might not occur to the thinking of your average officer.

"Look around you, my lord. This cellar is clearly of older and finer construction than the structure upstairs, and it's at least half again bigger. The original structure was no doubt stone as well, stone and timber, and it burned. If my lord will look up there, near the ceiling, he still can see the fire marks. That structure was never rebuilt, but its foundation, including this cellar, was used for the brickwork house still standing."

"What," demanded Vakos, "has all this to do with our elusive murderer, lieutenant?"

With a languid, assured smile, the officer replied, "Please bear with me, my lord. Now, when these frontier cities were built, often the citadels and walled mansions were completed before the city walls even were commenced. So, since the residents and garrisons were often in constant danger of barbarian attack, they frequently devised ways of communicating one with the other, of getting supplies or reinforcements to hard-pressed areas quickly and safely, of—"

Vaskos' big fist smacked into his horny palm and his

black eyes flashed. "*Tunnels*! Of course! That's why we've never caught the bastard, or even seen him, despite streets crowded with patrols. I must be getting senile, lieutenant. I should have thought of it ere this."

Young Gahloopohlos showed a rueful grin. "Then I fear I must share my lord's senility, for even with my experience, I gave no thought to the matter until it slapped me in the face."

Vaskos nodded brusquely. "Well, we know now, good Gahloopohlos. It sounds reasonable to me. Let us get a squad down here with sledges and bars, get these stones down and see if we're right."

The officer shook his head. "Such measures are unnecessary, my lord. You see?" Sidling to a section of wall which looked no different from many other sections about the cellar, he placed both hands flat upon it and, bunching his body behind his shoulders, heaved. His feet slid back on the rough flooring as the wall section briefly resisted his strength, but then, with a ponderous grinding and a shriek of seldom-used metal, a man-length of wall swiveled to reveal a stygian-black rectangle from which emanated the cold, dank smell of sunless earth.

Vaskos waited for the arrival of additional men before he, Ahlee, the lieutenant and a squad of soldiers filed into the narrow tunnel. Only a few steps did they proceed, however, for the way was blocked by a mound of earth and chunks of soft, rotten timber. An aperture no more than two feet wide or high had been dug through the blockage, and there they found more blood and another shred of the same fine woolen.

There was another wait, for not liking the look of the extant shoring, Vaskos had some of the soldiers repair the areas above and return with odds and ends to strengthen the worm-eaten boards and columns. Then, one at a time, holding their torches before them, the officers, the physician and a dozen men wriggled through the ten terrible suffocating feet of crumbling earth.

Beyond, the narrow tunnel continued for a few more paces, then entered at a right angle into a wider and better-shored tunnel which seemed to stretch infinitely away in two directions.

"Sun and Wind!" swore Vaskos, softly. "The bastard could have taken that poor woman in either direction.

There's nothing else for it but to split up. Gahloopohlos, you take six men and head that way. The master and I will take five and head the other. Sergeant Dahbzuhn, go back to the cellar and get the other squad, less two men to stand guard. You bring five after me and send five after the lieutenant. And sergeant, all of you, make no unnecessary noise until the quarry's in plain sight and, let's hope, at bay. He surely knows these tunnels better than we do, and we can't afford to miss him yet again."

Arrived in his cellar, Danos had gone through the joyless motions—stripping and gagging the half-conscious woman, then securing her ankles and wrists to a large rectangle of strong wooden construction. He had fabricated the rectangle many long months before, during the early days of the siege. With a victim's hands and feet lashed to its corners, the tenderest and most sensitive portions of the body were easily accessible to whip or knife, fingers or teeth, pincers or licking flame.

That detail attended to, he had employed the whip, pulping first the back, then turning the rectangle and its moaning, fainting occupant to lay open the tender breasts with the blood-wet lash. By this time, he should have been used to an audience, but he still was somewhat inhibited in his reactions by those darkly mad eyes staring from the corner; consequently, even when white ribs were showing through the lacerated, bleeding flesh of the woman's chest, he still felt no pleasant, stirring warmth in his loins. Not until he had leaned the rectangle against a wall and commenced to rain whistling blows on inner thighs and on the pudenda itself did he experience the tardy tumescence.

When he arose from the ravaged body, his loins now slack, he privately suspected the woman to be already dead or so near death as to make no difference, but warily he made no mention of the fact. After adjusting his clothing, the slick, black leather facings all wet and red-sticky, he drew his military dirk and expertly opened the upper abdomen. Leaving the dirk by the body, he stood up and stepped back.

"Dinner is served, my lord." He addressed the lurker in the shadowy corner. "I'm going above to watch for the patrol, as usual. Please signal when you've done, sir."

On his way up the littered stairs, Danos tried hard not to hear the slurping noises.

Ahlee had lost count of the numbers of small side tunnels his party had explored. Their original torches had already guttered out and, had the practical sergeant not thought to have the reinforcements carry extras, they would all now be fumbling about in utter darkness. The physician's jaws ached from the effort of keeping them clamped against the chattering of his teeth, for he like the rest found the dank chill of these passages harder to bear than the icy weather aboveground.

They had slowly proceeded up the left-hand side of the large tunnel, come at length to a blank wall of rough-hewn granite which Vaskos had opined to be probably the foundation of part of the city walls. Now they were working back down the other side. As Ahlee, moving just behind Vaskos and the sergeant, came abreast of yet another side tunnel, he became unpleasantly conscious of a palpable emanation of purest evil radiating from the depths of that narrow passage, its uncleanness and power making him sick and dizzy.

"Vaskos!" he whispered, croakingly, pulling at the burly officer's sleeve. "In there, I think. If not what we seek, at least something . . . something of terrible wrongness."

All the still-unblocked side tunnels were very similar in construction—twenty to thirty feet long, about six feet high and three wide—but the differences in this one were quickly apparent. The shoring was all new, the upper areas of it stained with torch soot, and they trod not bare earth but paving tiles . . . splotched here and there with dark brownish stains which clearly were not soot. A small chamber always lay at the cellar end of these side tunnels. This one contained a pile of fresh torches and a heap of torn and gore-stiffened rags which, on closer examination, proved to all be various articles of women's clothing.

Ahlee hoped that he would never again see such a look on his friend's face as Vaskos dropped a ripped, crusty shift, drew his sword and motioned for two soldiers to open the wall section which led to the cellar.

Some of these sections had been completely immovable, some had yielded only after long and difficult labor, but this one swung easily and noiselessly open . . . laying before their eyes a scene of unrelieved ghastliness.

The cellar was brightly lit by a couple of torches and several lamps. Warmth was provided by a pair of large braziers. His back to the newcomers, a man's figure crouched over the spread-eagled body of a gagged woman. Her wide-open eyes were death-glazed and set in a reflection of agony beyond endurance, horror beyond belief. What could be seen of her body and legs brought the sour bile bubbling up into Ahlee's throat, for all that he had closely examined so many cavaders with identical savageries imprinted in their cold flesh.

A red-smeared dirk was held loosely in the crouching man's right hand, while his left held what appeared to be a lump of fresh organ meat. While they watched—battle-hardened soldiers shocked into stillness and silence by the unnatural spectacle before them—the man drove the dirk into a timber of the blood-encrusted torture frame to which the dead woman's stiffening limbs were still bound, laid the piece of meat upon the pulpy red ruin which had been her breasts, did something with his freed hands, then bent his neck and lowered his head. The terrible sound which then smote their ears was that of beast, not of mankind. Of beast busily lapping!

Vaskos, too, sounded then like a beast, growling deep in his throat. He stalked forward, cat-light, his swordblade at low guard, ready for stab or slash. The sergeant and other soldiers advanced behind him, filling the width of the cellar from wall to wall with an inexorably moving wall of armored, steel-tipped bodies.

But the feeding beast heard the growls and shufflings as they neared him and whirled about, his pallid face and graying beard a single nauseous mask of clotting blood, madness glinting its evil from out his bloodshot black eyes, his broken and rotting red-stained teeth bared in a bestial snarl of rage. Jerking the dirk from the timber, he hurled himself at Vaskos, the foremost of these intruders.

His own lips skinned back in a grimace of savage joy, the officer set himself for a thrust. With a habitual stamp and shout, the long blade swept up and the muscular arm extended, but the sharp steel met empty air and Vaskos almost fell on his face on the blood-slick floor, whereon lay the suddenly senseless hulk of *Vahrohnos* Myros Deskati of Morguhn, but bare feet from the ravaged corpse whose liver he had torn out, whose blood he had been drinking.

Some two hours after these events, with the madman
once more securely manacled in his cell and guarded by
grim Regulars, Vaskos again sat behind his desk, glowering at Captain Danos. The former rebel officer's baldric
draped loosely, the cased sword it had held now hand-car-
ried by one of the husky guardsmen who flanked him. On
a cloth on the desk lay the partially cleaned dirk which
had been taken from the *vahrohnos* in that cellar of ter-
rors.

They had had the captain's story. Now Vaskos bluntly
spake his mind. "Captain, you are either a careless,
feckless fool or a cunning, glib-tongued monster. I confess
that I know not which, at this point. I'd like to think you
the latter, but that's because I hate you for reasons that
you well know.

"The fact that this dirk fits your empty case really
proves nothing, since both are Confederation Army issue.
Your charge lies comatose in his cell, so it will be days ere
we can question him. Not that that exercise will prove
anything either, for I'd not convict even such as you on
the unsupported word of a madman.

"You were found sleeping in your room here at the Citadel, and were nowhere seen on the streets tonight, but
neither fact absolves you, since I now am aware that there
exists a true warren of tunnels connecting the Citadel and
various quarters of the city.

"However, I have put my staff to checking the
presumed dates of the recent series of murders and questioning your men as to which nights you took the watch
over the *vahrohnos*. If the two lists coincide, captain, I
will assume that you are guilty, if not of duplicity, at least
of dereliction of your sworn duties. And that will make
me very happy, captain. My father, Lord Hari, and I were
denied our just vengeance on your flesh because you were
an amnestied officer fulfilling what the High Lord felt to
be a valuable function. You cannot be punished for the
crimes done in Morguhn, but damn you, I can damned
well court-martial you for those things you've done or not
done whilst under *my* command."

Then, to a guards officcer who stood stiffly by the door,
"Captain Nahks, the prisoner's quarters are to be thoroughly searched and all weapons are to be removed from

them. Then he will be there confined, with the door bolted and two men to guard it around the clock. Nor is anyone save myself or Master Ahlee to be allowed through his door. See that he is provided a jug of wine and a few rounds of barracks bread; that should serve him until I have enough information to issue you further orders. Now, take him away."

Chapter XI

The camp outside the walls of Vawnpolis first swelled monstrously with the influx of the troops who had been patrolling the border and manning the border forts, then shrank to even smaller limits than its original size as regiments and lesser units took the road for the long march back to Kehnooryos Ehlahs and the sprawling garrison city at Goohm. Hardly were the last of those on their way when most of the Confederation cavalry brigade jingled down from the western mountains to collect the baggage left behind at the commencement of the campaign and spend a few weeks resting and reorganizing.

Sub-*keeleeohstos* Gaib Linstahk, now commander of the Fifth *Kahtahfrahktoee*, eventually made time to call on his old friend *Strahteegos* Vaskos Daiviz. The preceding summer, while he still commanded only three troops of dragoons, his unit had been sent with Vaskos and Lord Hari to reclaim Horse County of the Duchy of Morguhn for the Confederation. As Gaib's own sire was a Kindred horse breeder, the three noblemen had easily and quickly become fast friends.

Vaskos was hard at work when his adjutant announced that a field-grade cavalry officer was in the outer office and requested a few words with the commander of Vawnpolis. What with the various comings and goings of so many units within the environs of the city, Vaskos had endured an endless succession of duty calls. As commander of Vawnpolis, he was the titular senior officer for all of Vawn, and courtesy calls were unavoidable, since no astute major or colonel or *keeleeohstos* would pass through without taking the opportunity to congratulate Vaskos on his promotion and do a bit of sly apple-polishing at the same time. So Vaskos never inquired this most recent caller's name or actual rank, nor did he bother to glance up when, with a jingling and jangling, the measured footfalls crossed from the door to a heel-clicking halt before his desk and a fist clanged on breastplate in formal salute.

"My lord *strahteegos*, please accept the heartfelt congratulations of all the officers and troopers of *Pehmptos Kahtahfrahktoee*, as well as those of their commander, Sub-*keeleeohstos* Gaib Linstahk, who is my lord's servant in all honorable ways."

Vaskos had peremptorily returned the salute, though his eyes still were fixed on his work. His hand moved back toward his quill pen but stopped abruptly, as the familiar voice penetrated where the maddeningly familiar stock phrases would not. His scarred face suddenly split by a broad grin, he came to his feet, heedless of the heavy chair which crashed over behind him, and rounded the desk to greet Gaib with an armor-crushing hug of sincere welcome.

With the backslappings and informal, half-insulting felicitations done, Vaskos shouted for his adjutant and soberly promised thirty lashes to anyone who disturbed him with anything less earthshaking than an investment of Vawnpolis or the arrival of the High Lord; then he bolted his door and brought in his hidden jar of honeywine.

As they sat before the hearth with its fire of hard, bluish coal lumps, Vaskos studied his young friend critically. The cares and worries of command had already begun to leave their unmistakable marks upon the handsome, weather-dark face—furrowed brow, crinkled eyecorners and the beginning of the hard lines at the corners of the mouth, as well as the dark crescents under bloodshot eyes which Vaskos knew he shared. It seemed that the higher an officer's rank, the less sleep he could count on getting of a night.

But there were other marks visible, as well. A pink pucker of scar now ran from just below the bridge of the nose to the angle of the jaw, and the smallest finger was missing from Gaib's bridle hand. For all that returning Freefighters chortled over an all but unopposed foray, it was clear that the *kahtahfrahktoee* had seen some hard fighting.

When he had stuffed the clay bowl of a Zahrtohguhn waterpipe, Vaskos' callused fingers lifted a tiny coal from the hearth, dropped it atop the fragrant tobacco and puffed until it was going well. Then he handed the other mouthpiece to Gaib.

"Master Ahlee, the physician, you remember him? Well, he gifted me with this contraption. Says that, if smoke I must, this is the only good way to do it. The container, here, is filled with brandy, you see, and the smoke is cooled and flavored by it. I must admit, I've gotten quite fond of the bastard."

Gaib blew a smoke ring toward the ceiling and smiled. "You don't know, truly, how good it is to see you again, Vaskos, or how relieved I am to find that the lord commander of Vawnpolis still is the friend I came to know last summer."

Vaskos' brow wrinkled in puzzlement. "Why shouldn't I be, Gaib?"

The cavalryman slapped at the cuff of his jackboot. "Sun and Wind, Vaskos, you've been a soldier nigh on thirty years; you've seen it. Breathing the rarefied air granted to *strahteegoee* has turned more heads than one, and we both know it. But it's always good to see the men who can carry high rank with dignity rather than arrogance. You're a fine man and officer as you are, lord *strahteegos*, and I'm right proud to call you friend. Were you to metamorphose into one of those strutting, supercilious popinjays that seem to abound in the capital, and sometimes deign to come out to Goohm. I might be some loath to admit I know you."

"Scant chance of that, m'boy." Vaskos took a long draft of wine and grinned. "I weren't yet sixteen when I enlisted, as a common spearman, and my highest ambition in those days was to make senior sergeant. But then some fool officer took me under his wing an' groomed me proper and next I knew I was a sergeant cadet. Four years later he had me shipped off to Bloozburk an' here I be. But I'm still that senior sergeant I never got to be, Gaib. Down under, that's all I'll ever be, I s'pect."

His grin returned then. "But tell me some war stories, Gaib. Tell me about the female who bit off that finger, for instance. For the sake of your lord father, I hope that was *all* she managed to bite off." He chuckled.

Gaib shook his red-blond head ruefully. "For all I can say, some Ahrmehnee did bite the pinky off. I have no memory of receiving the wound, none at all. It wasn't until everything was done that I even realized it was gone."

Vaskos nodded. "Oh, yes, that's happened to me, too. Happens to most men—you get into a skirmish and—"

Gaib shook his head, grimly. "This was no skirmish, old friend. It started as a surprise attack, became a full-scale battle and might well have been a near rout, but for the incredible bravery of my lord Drehkos and a few score of his rebels, who—"

Vaskos' scarred face darkened and there was dull anger in his voice as he growled, "Friend Gaib, amnestied he may be, but to my father and me, he will always be a despicable traitor, and we'll hear nothing of him, now or in the future."

"Oh, no, friend Vaskos," Gaib disagreed. "Like it or not, you and your father will hear of, and probably from, the Lord Drehkos for the rest of your life." He leaned forward and lowered his voice conspiratorily. "You must respect the confidential nature of what I am about to tell you, Vaskos, for it's not yet common knowledge in the expeditionary force. Indeed, I'd not be aware of it myself but that I was once of the Bodyguards and still have many old friends amongst them.

"Vaskos, your Uncle Drehkos led the heroic defense of our camp that morning, unarmored. His few score rebels fought and held, briefly, two or three thousand Ahrmehnee, and almost all of that scratch force took their death wounds, including your uncle, who was run through the body with a wolfspear."

"Good riddance," Vaskos snarled, "to bad rubbish!"

A restrained awe entered the younger officer's tone. "But, Vaskos, the Lord Drehkos did not die! He pulled out the spear and by the next morning was sitting his horse beside the High Lady on the march. And she has kept him at her side since."

Vaskos' cup clattered onto the hearth and rolled, hissing and unheeded, into the fire. His widening eyes starting from his suddenly pallid face, he croaked, "Gaib . . . man, do you *know* what you're implying?"

Gaib nodded. "No implication, that, old friend. The guardsmen say that the High Lord and the High Lady have administered every test and both now are satisfied that the Lord Drehkos, your esteemed relative, is *of the Undying.*"

"And I say, hogwash!" shouted Vaskos. "Man, my uncle is two years younger than my father and *looks* a good ten years older. My father, and many another in Morguhn, have known the man all his misspent life. There's just no way you could possibly have heard the truth."

Gaib flavored his reply with a humorless smile. "I thank you for not putting the lie into my mouth, at least. But, Vaskos, I talked with guardsmen who assisted in the tests, some of them, anyway. With your uncle's free consent, dirk blades were thrust into his body rendering fatal wounds, and still he lived. The Lord Milo and the Lady Aldora both are satisfied, why should you not be?"

With the first, green shoots of spring, the High Lord led the last of his regiments down from the western mountains, leaving Fort Kohg—as the castra was now called in honor of the *nahkhahrah*—manned by a mixed force of Confederation volunteers and native Ahrmehnee warriors, all under the command of Senior *Strahteegos* Hahfos Djohnz, who now bore the additional title of Lord Warden of the Ahrmehnee Marches, his actions accountable to none save the *nahkhahrah* and Milo.

At the High Lord's side rode the *nahkaharah*, well pleased with what he had, and would, accomplish for his people. Also, he was pleased that the Lord Milo had chosen Hahfos to be deputy. He felt his people would come to truly love the wise and competent but quiet and unassuming officer, and now that Hahfos was safely wed, by Ahrmehnee rites, to a girl of the Bahrohnyuhn Tribe, he was more or less Ahrmehnee himself. And, the old man mused on, if the Lady did not choose to grant children to him and his own new wife, there could be no complaint from any tribe were he to name as his successor Lord Hahfos' firstborn son.

While Drehkos Daiviz, still a little unbelieving that he was truly Undying, listened, Aldora was patiently explaining to the Lady Zehpoor Taishyuhn, new wife of the *nahkhahrah*, the precise stations of her and her husband.

"Of the First Rank, there be but three—though there will be four as soon as we reach the capital and dear Drehkos is confirmed a High Lord. Of the Second Rank are such as foreign kings, princes, *kahleefahee*, and the like. The Third Rank includes such foreign titles as grand duke, or archduke, both of which are the same as our own *ahrkeethoheeks*; senior *strahteegoee* hold this rank as long as they remain in the army, as do certain high officials of the Confederation.

"Since the High Lord has decided that your husband will be *ahrkeethoheeks* of the Ahrmehnee, he and you will be of the Third Rank, officially. But, actually, you and Kogh are much more valuable to us than any score of *ahrkeethoheeksee*."

Zehpoor looked puzzled. "But, my lady, all of the Ahrmehnee *Stahn* cannot raise ten thousand warriors, so I cannot understand—"

"Milo and Mara and I, Zehpoor, are very interested in the many and widely diverse powers of the mind. We have devoted many years of study to them and have even established an academy of sorts to see if people lacking them can be taught to . . . to . . . well, to control their minds sufficiently to unleash powers they did not know they had. Milo can explain the aims of the Academy far better than can I."

At a wider place in the trail, Drehkos reined aside and allowed the column to proceed past him until he spied his brother, *Komees* Hari, at the head of his mixed force of Freefighters, nobles and Moon Maidens. Then he toed his horse out to ride at his brother's side.

Some week or so after the Night of Fire, Hari and young Sir Geros had led three hundred riders to the castra, having missed the *nahkhahrah's* village by dint of faulty maps. With them had come two Ahrmehnee women, to whom Captain Pawl Raikuh owed his life. Many of the column were wounded when they arrived and all were near starvation. Nonetheless, the old *komees* had lost no time in reporting to the High Lord. And he had been too exhausted even to protest the presence of his despised brother in the High Lord's pavilion.

He had detailed the highlights of the forced march, the finding of Raikuh's butchered force, the approach to and advance onto the plateau. He told of the ruined village and its cruelly massacred inhabitants, then of the witnessed stand of the Ahrmehnee warriors and Moon

Maidens against the thousands of barbarians and their monstrous leader.

At that point, the *nahkhahrah* had interrupted. "Your pardon, sir. Did you hear this creature addressed, by chance? If so, what was he called?"

Hari shrugged tiredly. "No, I heard nothing addressed to the giant. But some of the Maidens who rode in with me have mentioned that the Muhkohee's leader was one Buhbuh."

The *nahkhahrah* nodded. "Thank you, sir." Then he turned to Milo. "I have never heard of one of that name, though it is a common name amongst the Muhkohee. But this leader your officer describes can be only one of the terrible monsters of whom I told you, the Haidehn Tribe. Since most of them are powerful sorcerers, they are the richest of all the Muhkohee, but they are also cannibals, and no more evil tribe has ever stalked Our Lady's earth!"

"Well, sorcerer or not, he soon found his Northorse couldn't outrun Bili's Mahvros," said Hari, grimly. "Nor did either magic or armor keep that great axe out of his flesh. Bili smote him out of the saddle and our squadron rode over his body."

The *nahkhahrah* grunted his approval. Milo asked, "Bili routed near three thousand men with one under-strength squadron, then?"

Hari's grin was fierce with pride, though pain was in his eyes. "Aye, my lord, Duke Bili sent the Freefighter bow-masters, under command of Count Taros Duhnbahr of Baikuh, around to the top of the cliff against which the warriors and Maidens were standing at bay. Then, when the barbarian bastards already were reeling under the ar-row rain, he led the rest of the squadron athump into their right flank, while my wing took them in the rear. And these little ponies just aren't built to take the charge of a good warhorse, my lord. Even so, it was a near thing once the momentum of the charge was lost and the squadron was fragmented.

"But then Duke Bili rallied most of us, reformed, rein-forced by Count Taros' bowmasters along with several troops' worth of Maidens and Ahrmehnee, and hit the en-emy in the left flank. That second charge did it, my lord—they broke and fled southwest, down the slope of that plateau, with us in hot pursuit.

"And we ran them, my lord. What a chase that were! Kindred and Freefighters and cats, Moon Maidens and Soormehlyuhn warriors, we chivvied and harried the bastards clear to the end of the bloody plateau. I never got the chance to ride back over the route and the battlefield, but I trow not five hundred got away. And we might've got more had Bili not stopped the pursuit when he did.

"It was while we were riding back—rather, most of us were walking to spare the horses—that the earthquake struck. Since the quake seemed to be coming from the north and since the plateau was obviously unsafe, what with the broken ground and all, we were mostly happy to follow Duke Bili down and off it. But the face we came down started to break up before the tail of the column was clear, my lord, and there weren't much room at the bottom, so we took off in two directions; me with the force I brought in, Duke Bili with maybe two hundred.

"When it was over, when the ground stopped shaking and rumbling and when those hot rocks stopped falling, I led my group back and found the end of the plateau had broken up and slid down into a little vale. What of the rest of the plateau we could see looked to be all afire, and that cliff where the Maidens and Ahrmehnee had made their stand had disappeared completely. It was more burning forest southeast and southwest, and given the poor condition of my force, I felt it unwise to take them into that inferno, put them in more danger. I knew that Duke Bili, too, had maps and I assumed he would find his own way north."

He shook his head sadly. "Now I wonder if I erred, my lord. Perhaps . . . ?"

"Not a bit of it, *Komees* Hari," snapped the High Lady Aldora. "You made a command decision, did what you thought best for the troops under you. Considering the circumstances and the conditions you've outlined, I doubt me I'd have done differently. Don't berate yourself further. I'd say you had no choice."

Hari's relief had flooded his lined face. That Aldora, who was not only Bili's lover but a recognized authority on cavalry tactics, could thus absolve him of blame lifted a weighty load from his loyal old conscience. He continued then.

"It took us near two days, my lord, to backtrack to

where we had gone onto the plateau. But the gap had fallen in. Sir Geros climbed atop the tumbled rocks and returned to say that he had seen precious little, since all the land in both directions seemed covered with a thick blanket of smoke, even the tops of the hills and ridges. So, with our supply train gone, too, I decided our best course was to hotfoot it north while still we could travel."

Draining off the last of his welcome cup, Hari stood and said, "Now, my lord, I'd like to tell of another matter. When the main barbarian force all but annihilated Captain Raikuh's squadron, the captain was seriously wounded but still managed to stay on his horse for some little distance though pursued closely by a number of the savages. Finally, the pain and loss of blood so weakened him that he fell and the horse ran on without him. That horse came into my camp later that night; it was the first sign we had that ill had befallen Raikuh's command.

"Raikuh says he was lying there, too weak even to feel for his dirk, hearing the approaching yells of the barbarians, when, suddenly, an Ahrmehnee woman stepped out of the forest onto the trail ahead of him. He says he tried to tell her to get back into hiding, but she just stood there serenely, ignoring him.

"Then the knot of shaggy riders swept around the turn, and Raikuh knew he'd fought his last battle. But then they stopped so suddenly that the leading ponies reared and several of the rear rank rode into them. All the while, the woman had just been standing in the trail, a few paces ahead of him, and he'd expected the shaggies to just cut her down and go for him.

"But they cast several darts, well over her head, then jerked their ponies' heads about and rode out of there as if a regiment of dragoons had been on their tails; some of them were actually screaming. When their hoofbeats faded, the woman shouted something and another woman came out of the forest and the two of them came over to where Raikuh lay.

"At first they tried carrying him, but the weight was too much. So they put him down and, with what little help he could give them, got most of his armor off. Then they half carried and half dragged him into the forest and over a hill and into a little cave—really, just a deep rock overhang."

Komees Hari spun a good tale. Aldora, the *nahkhahrah*, Senior *Strahteegos* Hahfos Djohnz, everyone within hearing, sat rapt. And Milo remembered the long centuries on the Sea of Grass, when Daiviz bards had been renowned as the best and most creative storytellers.

The inheritor of that ancient art continued. "Now, Raikuh's been soldiering most of his life, and he's near my own age, so he knows what death wounds look like and he knew he had at least two of them, knew that he'd not last the night. So when the older woman—the one what had faced down the barbarians—gave him something to drink, he figured it would be near his last drink.

"My lord, Raikuh swears his Sword Oath on what I'm going to tell you now, and he's not a man to lie on his Sword. When he woke up, the Sun was shining and he not only wasn't dead, he wasn't even in very much pain! Somehow, my lord, that older woman—he's pretty sure it was her, since the other's but a girl and seems the elder's helper—had got *two* iron dartpoints out of Raikuh's vitals, *while he slept*, and had sewn up the flesh with sheepgut as neatly, I trow, as could any Zahrtohguhn physician."

The High Lord nodded. "The Confederation owes those women a debt of gratitude. Captain Raikuh is a valuable officer and has served us well. I take it, *Komees* Hari, that those are the ones who rode in with your group. How did you come across them?"

"According to that damned map, my lord, we were too far west to hit the village where Duke Bili'd said we were to meet you if we headed straight north, so we backtracked down the trail we'd advanced up. We'd come up at a pretty fair rate of march, with point and flanks scouted by the cats. Well, all the cats went with Bili, so we marched slower and more careful coming back, and Sir Geros came across Raikuh's armor and recognized it, since the two of them had been good friends for near on a year.

"When he reported his find to me, I knew the savages hadn't gotten him, for they never leave hardly a scrap of anything except dead bodies on a field they win. So I fanned out parties to both flanks and we started looking for his corpse. A squad of Maidens stumbled onto the cave and explained the situation to the two women. And, my lord, that was that."

"What has the *nahkhahrah* to say on this matter?" the High Lord inquired politely.

"There are a few wise women among the Ahrmehnee, Lord Milo," Kohg had replied. "Never very many in any one generation. Since they conduct mostly women's rites, few men know much concerning them. Few of these wise women ever marry, so they choose a girl from among whatever tribe they serve and train her to their craft. Though the wise women instruct midwives and tribal healers, they seldom perform such work themselves. Nonetheless, I have heard of some quite remarkable cures certain of them have wrought, over the years. It is said that they have the power to literally thrust their hands through flesh, without breaking the skin or drawing any blood, and remove tumors or foreign objects from the body. Understand me, Lord Milo, I've never *seen* it done, but I *know* that it has been done."

Milo and Aldora exchanged a glance, then he addressed *Komees* Hari. "I'd like to meet this wise woman, Hari. Have her sent for."

The old nobleman smiled. "I thought my lord might. She awaits his pleasure in the next chamber."

Milo guessed the age of the woman Hari ushered in at something under forty. He thought, too, that she must have been a raving beauty at twenty; even now, she was a handsome, high-breasted creature. Nor did she appear abashed in this august gathering. She strode gracefully at Hari's side, seemingly oblivious of her rumpled, travel-stained garments, the ghost of a smile tugging at her full, dark-red lips. Her black eyes locked briefly with the *nahkhahrah's* and Milo saw the old man start as if stabbed, but neither spoke and Milo felt it impolitic to pry.

Then her sloe-black gaze met Milo's and he found her mindspeak as powerful as his own. "Zehpoor greets you, Ageless One. I am glad that the Ahrmehnee are no longer your enemies. But, friend or foe, I can tell *you* nothing of my Powers or of how they be wrought. For this be woman's magic, not men's, and it is not Our Lady's will that I betray my Sacred Vows to Her . . . at least, not those Vows regarding healing."

"I respect both your oaths and your silence, my lady," beamed Milo. "But—"

The smile fully flowered as she silently interrupted. "But still are you rabid for more knowledge of my Powers, Milo of Morai. It is our Lady's will that you shall have that knowledge—all that knowledge—but not of my revealing, not directly. The Lady Mara, that lovely, Ageless Ehleen woman you consider wife, will receive of me and transmit to you, since she is not Avowed.

"You will do much of good with that knowledge, both in this land and in that land to which you will, one day, lead the distant descendants of those who now serve you."

A strong shudder coursed through Milo's every fiber and he felt an icy prickling on his nerve ends. Aldora had been receiving as well, and now she mindspoke him.

"Yes, Milo, I feel it too. That eerieness, it . . . it's as if dear old Blind Hari of Krooguh were speaking through her lips." Then she beamed to the woman, saying, "When did you scan our futures, my lady, and why?"

Zehpoor answered readily. "No shade of a sightless Man of Powers speaks through me, Ageless Lady, nor did I purposely scan your futures. Rather did Our Lady reveal to me the future of the girl, Pehroosz, whom She led to my keeping. The threads of that future and of the futures of her children's children's children are closely tied to those of you Ageless Ones." She paused, then added, "But of these things, too, Milo of Morai, you will know when it is Her will that you know."

Milo's lips smiled thinly and fleetingly. "All right, Lady Zehpoor, I'll await the pleasure of your goddess on the bulk of these matters, but at least show me how you, a lone and unarmed female, managed to scare the wits out of the Muhkohee. According to the *nahkhahrah*, here, their ilk doesn't take fright easily."

Though Drehkos's mindspeak was daily strengthening, it still was not on a par with those deathless two who had used it for hundreds of years, nor was it a match for that of the gifted Zehpoor, therefore he had received only bits and pieces of the silent exchanges and was utterly unprepared for what followed.

The lissome figure of the drably clad woman wavered before her audience. Then, all in the blinking of an eye, she was replaced by the awesome form of a monstrous bear, looming threateningly over *Komees* Hari, who was momentarily petrified with shock. Huge and horrible, black as nightmare, the sow bear stood on hind legs thick as treetrunks. Yellowish fangs gnashed and baleful red eyes flashed pure, blood-lusting menace from that gigantic head which brushed the very ridgepole—more than twelve feet above the floor. The apparition shuffled slowly forward, the long, needle-tipped claws of the forepaws lowering relentlessly toward Hari.

On the other side of the table, only the *nahkhahrah* had remained in his chair. Even Milo and Aldora, who had been expecting something of the sort, found themselves on their feet, steel bared, standing crouched to receive the attack.

But not so Drehkos! He was up and over the table, both sword and dirk out. His shoulder struck his brother with force, knocking him prone. "Get under the table, Hari!" he snapped. "It can't really harm me, but it can kill you." Then he sent the heavy dirk spinning straight for one of those satanic eyes, ducked under the threatening forepaws, and—

The bear was gone and Drehkos's sword was stabbing the air above the head of Zehpoor. The close bond which had been the brothers' from boyhood to the rebellion had resumed from that hour.

Therefore, as they rode down from the mountains, Hari greeted Drehkos warmly, unabashed by the knowledge that this man, his younger brother, was immortal. "Come slumming, have you?" he joshed. "You've then tired of the life of an Undying God, already? What'll you do for your next fifty-odd years, brother mine?"

Drehkos did not return the smile. "Both Milo and Aldora tried to farspeak Bili last night, Hari, and they could neither of them range his mind. And that bodes ill. That bodes exceedingly ill. Who is Bili's heir? Djef Morguhn, isn't it?"

"No, Drehkos," Hari sighed. "Young Djef died at the siege of Morguhn Hall, last year. Tchahrlee be next eldest, and he be already holding the duchy as deputy *thoheeks* . . . but, dammit, Drehkos, I can't tell you why, but . . . but I just don't think Bili's dead."

Drehkos made the Sun-sign before his face. "I pray Sacred Sun you be right, brother Hari."

Hari reached over to touch Drehkos's skin and mind-spoke on a strictly personal level. "And, Undying Brother,

I am not alone in my faith in Bili's ability to survive. Last night, Sir Geros Lahvoheetos and Pawl Raikuh rode southwest, along with fourscore Freefighters of the old Morguhn Troop, twice that number of warriors of the Soormehlyuhn Tribe and thirty-four of the Moon Maidens who rode north with me.

"I'm prepared to swear that I knew nothing of their intended desertion until they were long gone, Drehkos. Candidly, however, I did all I could to see them well provided, well armed and well mounted. And they know, too, that they ride with my blessing. Sun and Wind grant those brave men success, I say, for Duke Bili is a man in a million, Steel keep him."

Chapter XII

It had been full night before Kogh and Zehpoor had had the opportunity to find a place apart. His first words were simple and blunt.

"It is really you then, Zehpoor Frainyuhn?"

She had smiled a little sadly. "Yes, father-in-law-who-might-have-been, I am Zehpoor of the Tribe of Frainyuhn, daughter of Kehroon. How . . . how is Behdrohz, your son?"

"He is dead these twenty years, child, killed on a raid against the Duhnkin *Stahn*. They all told him that *you* were dead, Zehpoor. Your father showed him your grave. Why were we so deceived?"

The woman hung her head, half-whispering. "I am so very sorry, *Der* Kogh, so very very sorry. But my poor father had no choice. Mother Djainoosh announced suddenly that she had chosen me. She would not relent even when she was told it was your son I was promised to. What else could my father do?"

His arm went about her shoulders in a gentle embrace. "Nothing but what he did do, child. Do not grieve, I understand, and I am certain that my fine, brave Behdrohz would have, too. I can but regret that he is not here to see how lovely is that woman I choose to bear my grandchildren. The Taishyuhns would have made you both welcome and happy, Zehpoor."

The lamplight glinted from her hair as she raised her head. "And does that welcome still stand, *nahkhahrah*?" A faint smile tugged at her lips. "Would still Zehpoor Frainyuhn be made happy in the Taishyuhn Tribe?"

"Why . . . why, of course, child, if you wish to give up your Vows. I have no sons left to wed you, but the winter has been hard and there are certain widowers . . ." His high forehead crinkled in concentration. "Let's see, there is a man, a *hetman* of a large, prosperous village. He is a raider of some renown and his house is rich with his spoils. Though he was one of my Behdrohz's cronies, age sits lightly on him and he is a strong and lusty man, he—"

She shook her head forcefully. "Not good enough."

"Well," the *nahkhahrah* tugged at his earlobe, "he's not a Taishyuhn, but I know of a *dehrehbeh* who recently lost a wife. But he be an older man."

Pushing herself away from him, she gazed levelly into his eyes. "It is not right that I should toy with you; credit the fact that I have to my woman's nature.

"On the night of the day the Bahrohnyuhn girl came to me, all bruised and ravaged by the lowlander raiders, I put her to the healing sleep and saw to her hurts. Then I ate the Sacred Plant and sojourned with Our Lady. She allowed me to see the futures She willed, among them my own.

"Kogh Taishyuhn, Our Lady wills that I repay old debts, so far as I now can. I am to remain faithful to all my Vows, save one. She will preserve me in my Powers only if I give the virginity, once pledged to her, to the *dehrehbeh* of the Taishyuhn Tribe."

"Zehpoor, child, I am a very old man. That son of mine to whom you were betrothed was the last child ever I sired, and his mother was the third wife I buried. His sister, who has ordered my house and slaves for about fifteen years, is herself almost old enough to be your mother, so it is most doubtful that I can quicken you, as a good husband should."

She just smiled. "That doesn't matter, Kogh Taishyuhn."

"Of course it matters, Zehpoor. What use is a marriage if it does not produce children? Our Lady would be the first to—"

She continued to shape her lips in a smile, but her voice hardened perceptibly. "You have often spoken for Her, Kogh Taishyuhn, but you do not now. *I* speak Her will, Her desires, Her commands, this time. I am to render up to you that which was long ago promised your tribe, not because I so desire, but because I am so bidden. As regards age, I am no spring chicken, Kogh, and I cannot say that I honestly wish to undergo a carriage and birthing, especially not a first one, at my age. But I am Hers and must bow to Her Holy Will. You, too, are Hers, Kogh, by your man's rites, and you must add your own submission to mine."

"But who," the *nahkhahrah* demanded stubbornly, "is there to marry us? There now is no Taishyuhn older than am I."

She nodded once. "True, Kogh, true. But the *stahn* is wisely become part of a larger *stahn*. And the *nahkhahrah* of this Confederation has at least ten times your moons."

Again would he have spoken, but she raised a finger. "No, Kogh, husband-to-be, hear me out. This Milo of Morai will say the words, taking those words and the proper usages from your mind. We will be joined three days hence, in the splendor of Her Newness.

"And soon, shortly after Her next Newness, you will perform the rites for Pehroosz Bahrohnyuhn and him who is war chief of the Ageless One's hosts. And the issue of that marriage will heap glory and honor upon both Confederation and Ahrmehnee *Stahn*, though we two will not live to see."

And he was too wise a man to think his stubbornness could prevail over the will of the Goddess. He bowed his snowy head and made the Moon-sign. Then he took the woman's head between his hands and pressed his lips tenderly to each closed eyelid, then to the full lips. Sitting back, he ritually squeezed her two breasts, then thrust his left hand far up beneath her skirt to make the Sacred Sign upon her pudenda.

"Thus, Zehpoor Frainyuhn, are you once more promised to the Taishyuhn Tribe. Your father is dead, child, so to whom should the brideprice be paid?"

"Give it to the *dehrehbeh* of Frainyuhn, Kogh, and tell him to equally divide it among my living brothers, keeping a share for himself." She extended a hand to touch him, then slowly and gingerly kneaded the swelling, throbbing flesh beneath her fingers. Smiling again, but now with a hint of mischief, she said, "Ah, Kogh, Kogh, I fear you have exaggerated your aged infirmity."

He returned her smile, placed his own hand over hers. "You are a lovely woman, Zehpoor, well formed and pleasing to both sight and touch." He hooked an arm about her waist and drew her closer to him, his other hand commencing another foray beneath her skirt.

For a moment, she seemed to melt, then she tore away

from him and came to her feet in one lithe movement. Her face flushed and, her high breasts rapidly rising and falling, her laughter trilled. "Oh, no, my Kogh, there'll be no sampling of the viands today. You . . . and I, too . . . must wait for the feast."

When informed of the coming nuptials, the younger Ahrmehnee warriors immediately embarked on a full-scale hunt for game. *Thoheeks* Hwahltuh Sanderz-Vawn and his bored clansmen joined in with a will, as did most of the civilian nobles and such Freefighters as attended them. But Milo doubted they would bag much, the winter having been both long and hard and the environs of the *stahn* much disturbed through movements of large bodies of troops and endless foragings. Therefore, he contributed a score of the herd of cattle he had had driven up from the lowlands, several hogsheads of wheaten flour, and ten full pipes of wine, plus many sacks of cornmeal and beans, dried fruits and vegetables, casks of cheeses and honey and salt, as well as barrel on barrel of that Confederation Army staple, shredded cabbage pickled with turnip and radish slices and garlic.

On the day before the festivities, Zehpoor called Pehroosz to her. Showing her some dried tubers, the older woman sketched the appearance of the plant whose roots they were and told Pehroosz the growing conditions favored by the plant. Then she gave Pehroosz a small wickerwork basket and a broad-bladed digging knife and sent her off into the wooded hills.

And after the girl was safely out of sight, Zehpoor surrendered to her tears. She had come to love the patient and cheerful, albeit sad-eyed, Pehroosz, and now she anguished at the terror the child would suffer this day. But she consoled herself: terror there would assuredly be, but no harm to Pehroosz, and much lasting good would come of that brief terror; and, besides, it was the Lady's will.

"It will do you good!" the High Lord had firmly stated, when he had ordered Senior *Strahteegos* Hahfos Djohnz to take part in at least the last day of the hunting. "You work too hard, Hahfos, and for too long at a time."

Hahfos thought it an example of the pot defaming the kettle, since there was seldom a night when the High Lord's pavilion wasn't brightly lit until well after the midnight hour. But when the High Lord finally lost patience and framed it as an order, Hahfos gave up and set about preparations.

Unlike the civilian noblemen, Hahfos had never been able to afford to maintain two or three horses. His destrier was a fine, well-trained warhorse, but a hunter he was not, so the officer rode up to the village and borrowed a shaggy, bony, piebald pony. He set out early in the day in company with a half-dozen middle-aged Ahrmehnee who thought they had seen signs of wild pigs within easy ride of the main village.

By midafternoon, the men were still sending their big hounds fanning out widely and vainly. But though they had flushed nary a porker, a shrewd cast of barbed dart had netted Hahfos a large, solitary stag. After his hunting companions had exclaimed over the size of the creature and the length and trickiness of the cast and had Hahfos red-faced in embarrassment at their blunt, jovial compliments, they all joined to speedily gut and bleed and clean the trophy and lash it across the back of the piebald gelding.

He rode the straining, overburdened little horse only until he was out of sight of his hosts, then dismounted and began to backtrail the earlier course at a brisk walk. While the pony sucked up water from an icy streamlet, Hahfos stood just downstream in the narrow, twisting defile and, with a wetted neckcloth, did what he could to remove dried sweat and deer's blood from his skin and clothing. It was then that the scream smote his ears, bouncing from wall to wall of the tiny vale, startling the drinking pony, who threw up his outsize head, snorting through wide-flared nostrils, though he was too tired and heavy-laden to bolt.

The women in the Taishyuhn villages had been in a whirl of activity since the announcement of the *nahkhahrah's* wedding date. Bread ovens glowed around the clock, while the flesh of butchered cattle, game and fowl needed immediate attention lest it begin to spoil. The hoards of charcoal were quickly exhausted, so a steady supply of wood was vital and the sound of the axe was almost constant in every village. No pair of hands could stay idle in such surroundings, nor had Pehroosz's. But the work was repetitious and she had been more than glad when Mother Zehpoor had sent her out of the village on her errand.

But a location of the sort described by the wise woman proved difficult to find, and her pony, too small and fine-boned to be taken for hunting, was frisky to the point of fractiousness; so that, when finally she chanced across a likely-looking spot, she was worn out with battling the strong-willed little horse.

She dismounted and tightly tied the reins to the trunk of a young maple, then took her basket and knife and proceeded to where a few mossy stones projected barely above the surface of an almost-circular deposit of deep loam, knelt and began to dig at the bases of a clump of the plants drawn by Mother Zehpoor.

When she had shaken the dark earth from the fleshy, finger-sized roots and put them in her basket, she probed the disturbed soil to be certain she had missed none of the tubers, since there appeared to be no more of the plants in the small area. But her knife sank only a bare inch into the loam when it was halted . . . and by something which did not feel like a stone or a tree root.

Wondering, she cleared away the shallow deposit to expose a dull, grayish surface, obviously metal, but unrusted and unlike any metal she ever had seen. Shoving aside the basket, she widened the excavation until she had the object free of dirt and roots. Then she squatted back on her heels and studied her discovery.

It was surely man-made; its even surfaces and sharp-angled corners were evidence of that fact. Pehroosz still could not identify the metal, for all that her mother's sister's husband had been the village smith and Pehroosz had had some little exposure to the sight of iron, various kinds of steel, brass, bronze, copper and even gold, silver and that mixture of the two called Ehleen-metal. Though this artifact bore a vague resemblance to silver, especially where her knife had cut through the dirt and oxidation, she was certain that it was not.

In size, it was about four spans of her hand across in either direction and half that in thickness. A couple of lines of what looked like some kind of lettering—though not in the Ahrmehnee language, Pehroosz knew, since she could write her name—were stamped across one side of the object, and another side sported what looked like a handle.

Leaning forward, Pehroosz sought to lift the artifact by that handle . . . and almost tumbled atop it. After long, hard effort, she at last managed to drag the weighty thing onto level ground. It seemed incredible that so small an item could be so heavy.

On the side which had rested on the bottom of the hole, she found yet another curiosity—a perfect circle of verdigris which, when carved away by her knife, revealed a disc of pitted bronze with a jagged slit, so narrow that her fingernail could barely enter it, centered in a round depression. Above this circle, a hair-fine seam ran from edge to edge across the face of the oddity. It was then that she concluded that she had found a chest of some kind, rather than simply a piece of old metal.

She decided to see if she could pry it open with her knife, but first arose to walk down to where she had tied her pony. The exertions had left her thirsty and a water bottle was tied onto the saddle. But her exertions had done more; the noise had awakened a nearby sleeper and, once awake, this sleeper was hungry, ravenously hungry.

Hahfos had left his fine, well-balanced darts with the Ahrmehnee hunters, but his wide-bladed boarspear was lashed to the pony's saddle. It was his only real weapon, since he had seen no need to burden himself with sword or dirk, replacing them with more practical saw-backed hanger and skinning knife. As a second terrified scream came hard on the heels of the first, this time blended with the scream of a pony or horse as well, he quieted his own mount enough to cast loose the lashings of the deer carcass. Throwing himself into the saddle, he drummed his heels on the little mount's barrel.

The defile twisted and turned and narrowed even more until, at its end, Hahfos was urging the pony through the stream itself. At the base of a small knoll, the water plunged into a dark hole, and the scream came yet again, from somewhere on the other side of that knoll. Hahfos put the game little piebald to the slope, leaning forward, his keen eyes searching the trees and underbrush above and his boarspear couched and ready.

Then he was among the trees at the summit and was almost unseated when his mount reared in terror at the edge of a tiny glade. Just across the open space, an Ahrmehnee girl clung ten feet up an ancient oak, splitting the air with her shrieks as a lean, cinnamon bear began to climb toward her.

The pony would go not one step closer, so Hahfos jumped from its back and ran to the base of the tree. Intent on filling his belly, the boar bear ignored the noises behind and below until several inches of sharp steel in his flesh made him aware that he was no longer necessarily the master of the situation.

Roaring his pain and fury, the big bear dropped from the trunk, spinning in midair to land facing his tormentor, who stood half-crouched, his bloody spear point held before him. Baring a mouthful of white teeth, the red bear charged.

Hahfos briefly regretted leaving his darts with the Ahrmehnee, as his dry tongue flickered over drier lips. He would have preferred the bear be at least crippled at rather a longer distance than five bare feet of spearshaft. But more than two decades of soldiering had taught him to accept those things impossible to change. Gritting his teeth, he set his feet solidly and braced himself for the coming trial of strength.

His arrival had been most fortuitous for Pehroosz. No sooner had her attacker ceased his stalking of her to do battle than the slender limb which had been supporting most of her weight snapped and her wails broke off abruptly when her soft rump smote the ground with sufficient force to drive the air from her lungs and set stars dancing in her head.

This bear was no cub; he had faced hunters before. He recognized the spear and its danger and dimly recalled the burning agony of suppurating spearwounds. Dropping to four feet, he came in low, presenting as little target as possible.

Hahfos's clenched jaws ached with strain, but he was unaware of the fact. All that now troubled him was the recollection of how Rehdjee, one of his older brothers, had died of the awesome wounds inflicted by a bear which had come in under his spear, as this one seemed intent upon doing. Taking a fearsome chance, the officer lowered his point, slashing its sharp edges at the animal's forelegs in the hope of forcing it erect so that he might have a chance at the heart.

The bear's roar changed timbre and gained volume as the keen steel bit into his off foreleg, just above the splayed, long-clawed paw. Lightning-fast, massive jaws closed upon the spearshaft, jerked so powerfully that Hahfos was certain his arms would be rent apart at the joints, then clamped down, splintering the two-inch hardwood shaft beneath the iron straps and so mangling the straps themselves that the head hung at a useless angle.

"How silly," thought Hahfos then, "to have survived so many years of war only to die under the claws and teeth of a dumb beast, while trying to protect a girl who, until a few weeks ago, was my enemy!"

For a few moments, the bear mauled the broken spear, attacking it so savagely that the head completely separated from the shaft Hahfos had dropped. In the space of those moments, the hard-pressed officer drew his single-edged hanger—better suited for dispatching and butchering beasts than for defending one's life—and set his back against the wide bole of a tall old tree.

To the girl, who looked to be just sitting on the ground across the clearing, he shouted, "*Run*, you witless little baggage! It'll not be long till he's done with me. Run to your pony, damn you, and ride like Sacred Wind!"

Then the bear was at him, all gnashing teeth and foul breath and raging fury. In his left hand, Hahfos grasped his cursive, pointless but razor-edged skinning knife. Choosing his moment shrewdly, he jammed the wide blade betwist the gaping jaws, hoping against hope that he might slice through enough muscles to render less effective those jaws and the fangs which were the bear's principal weapons. But a snapping of the jaws immobilized the knife before it had done more than deeply gash the tongue, and a jerk of the furry monster's head tore the hilt from Hahfos's grasp.

Pehroosz had not understood her savior's words, spoken in another language than her own, though his meaning had been unmistakable. But she was of a race of tough and hardy warriors and, seeing the stranger at bay against a treetrunk, his spear broken, facing a full-grown bear with only a clumsy-looking knife, she could not but try to aid him, even if her own life be forfeit.

The beast had reared onto his hind legs, which made him nearly Hahfos's full height. His furry chest was pressed tight against the man's leather jerkin, and only the hand gripping the throat under the slavering jaws and the straining muscles of the left arm had kept the blood-dripping teeth out of man flesh. The proximity of the antagonists, plus the protection afforded Hahfos by the treetrunk, made it impossible for the bear to make much use of his curving, needle-tipped claws, but this same proximity rendered the eighteen-inch hanger almost useless . . . and Hahfos could feel his straining thews weakening. He doubted he could hold back those jaws much longer.

Pehroosz staggeringly ran across the clearing, snatched up the four-foot remnant of spearshaft and began to belabor the beast's back and head and shoulders with the iron ferrule, but, though the concussions of her buffets increased her own dizziness, the bear took no notice of them. She finally stood back, panting. Her eyes, casting back and forth in search of a more effective weapon, lit upon the spearhead.

The boarspear is a weapon designed to the needs of a specific purpose—that of impaling a large, dangerous animal on a long and wide steel point, while a strong metal crossbar just behind the head prevents the wounded animal from impaling himself so far that he can get teeth or tushes or claws to the hunter. Unlike the lance, which is used for the much easier task of killing mere men, both edges of the spearhead are carefully honed to a razor keenness, so that slight movements of his shaft by an experienced hunter will slice away at the animal's internal organs, increasing hemorrhage and hastening death.

Pitting all her wiry strength to the task, Pehroosz drove the foot-long hand's-breadth of steel into the closest part of the bear's body. In the berserk rage of combat to the death, it is possible for man or beast to not even feel small injuries, but a leaf-shaped blade in the kidney is difficult to ignore. Tearing out of Hahfos's grasp, the bear whirled to face this new tormentor, and his heavy-muscled shoulder struck Pehroosz, sending her tumbling head over heels, consciousness leaving her in a great flash of blinding light.

But the respite, slight though it had been, was enough. Hahfos danced a halfstep to the side and, ere the roaring beast could turn back to him, the hanger had found and burst the mighty heart. When the stricken bear dropped to all fours, the roars suddenly replaced by pitiful, snuffling whimpers, Hahfos raised the heavy hanger high above his head and brought it whistling down to cleanly sever the spine, between shoulders and head, almost decapitating the dying bear.

Once sure that all life had fled the bloody carcass, the officer turned his attentions to the senseless girl, now bruised and bleeding from her violent contacts with mossy rocks and gnarled tree roots. Untying his still-damp neck-cloth, he knelt beside her and, cradling her rounded shoulders in the crook of his thick arm, wiped away what he could of the dirt and blood from her scraped and purpling cheeks and forehead. Then he gingerly began to feel and probe her limbs and body, searching for broken bones.

Half-conscious, Pehroosz's mind registered the cool moisture on her abraded face, but also the warmth of Hahfos's breath. Then hard hands were rubbing and kneading her body and, through slitted lids, a scarred, bristly face loomed waveringly above her. And she snapped into full consciousness. Screaming, sobbing in terror, she writhed to free herself from the man's grasp, her broken nails clawing at his eyes and cheeks, her small fists beating at his head and shoulders.

Thinking, naturally enough, that he was dealing with a simple case of post-combat hysterics, Hahfos deftly pinioned her lashing arms in one big hand and, rumbling calm, soothing, meaningless sounds, sought to enter her mind as he would have entered that of a frightened horse.

He entered Pehroosz's mind, entered as cleanly as a swimmer dives into still water, and what he found in her roiling, half-formed thoughts and in the murky depths of her memory shook the sensitive man to his innermost core. For Hahfos *was* a deeply sensitive man, feeling the sufferings of others even more keenly than he might his own, unswervingly believing in the innate goodness and dignity of men . . . and women. Not even a lifetime spent among scenes of harsh discipline, suffering and violent death had coarsened his basically gentle soul. The agonies and horrors the girl in his arms had endured tore at him, now, bred full-grown within him the resolve to shield her from further fright or pain so long as Sacred Sun continued to shine on his living body.

It was nearing dusk when Hahfos led the two ponies—Pehroosz and her strange casket on the one, the other tottering under the combined weights of the deer and the bear—into the square of the main village. Willing hands took the piebald's reins and set about unloading the carcasses, treating the officer to polite, but heartfelt, exclamations of joy at the sizes of the beasts, all couched in broken trade Mehrikan. Hahfos pleased them by using his steadily improving Ahrmehnee to thank them, then led Pehroosz's mount to the house she had indicated, in the doorway of which stood the sorceress who had saved Captain Raikuh.

The moon rode high when he delivered his charger to the horse handlers and strode the distance to his small pavilion. Fil, his orderly of many years, was there to take his commander's cloak, even while he eyed askance the bark-scraped jerkin under it.

"My lord had good hunting?" he inquired, draping the cloak over one arm, before reaching around Hahfos's trim waist to unbuckle the weapons belt. "Where are my lord's darts and spear? They will be in need of honing and greasing."

"Yes, Fil, the hunting was good. I bagged a deer and a bear. The darts I loaned to an Ahrmehnee gentleman. I'll bring them back tomorrow, after the wedding. The spear I left up in the hills—the bear chewed it to pieces."

Hahfos hurriedly unlaced his jerkin and, while pulling it over his head, mouthed a string of muffled orders. "Knowing you, old friend, you've had a great kettle of water seething since the last of day. Set up the trough, if you haven't already, and, while I'm bathing, you can lay out my second-best uniform, and the cat-helm, too. And send a guard to request an audience with the High Lord one half hour hence. Well, what are you waiting for, man? Let's hear those creaky bones moving!"

The High Lord left his place to stride over and wring Hahfos's hand, grinning merrily. "Of course you have my leave, Hahfos! And I wish you every happiness. Intermarriage has proven the only way to weld bonds between new lands and old. I had felt certain that some of the soldiers I'm going to leave to garrison this fort would wed

Ahrmehnee girls, but that you, one of my best officers
. . . " He suddenly smote fist in palm, exclaiming, "And
I'll gift you a wedding present, son Hahfos. You may have
personal choice of the men who make up the two battalions I'm leaving here. You'll command them, this fort
and the *stahn* as Lord Warden of the Ahrmehnee
Marches."

Hahfos reeled on suddenly weak legs, feeling a little as
if a warclub had smashed his helm. March wardens were
nobles of the *Third Rank*, the peers of *ahrkeethoheeksee*,
army marshals and lord councilors. He had never dreamed
of aspiring so high!

"And," the High Lord continued, "I'll even give you the
chit's brideprice."

Hahfos's color deepened. "Please, mah lord, no, mah
. . . mah lord is too generous."

"All right then," chuckled the High Lord, "call it a
loan. I'll hold your house and effects at Goohm as security."

The wedding of Kogh Taishyuhn to Zehpoor Frainyuhn
was completed in less than a quarter-hour, but the festivities stretched on for more than a week—dancing and
eating and dancing and guzzling and dancing and ritual
mock combats and dancing and a few deadly-serious combats and dancing and pony racing and dancing and more
gorging and guzzling, followed as a matter of course by
more dancing. Over the long centuries, Milo had been exposed to many different peoples and cultures, but he could
not recall another so obsessed with dancing. The village
and the sprawl of camps surrounding it resounded by day
and by night to the throbbings of Ahrmehnee drums, the
wails of flutes and the rhythmic stampings and clappings
and shouts of dancers and those who had stopped long
enough to cram their mouths with food or drain off gourds
of thick beer and tankards of wine.

Milo had thought it wise to keep most of his soldiers in
the castra, bringing no more than a score of officers and
men from each regiment. He still knew relatively little of
the Ahrmehnee, but he knew his soldiery in great detail
and had no wish to in any way endanger this unexpected
godsend of final peace with the fierce mountaineers who
had for so long plagued his border duchies.

But as it turned out, most of the Confederation troops

got to enjoy a bit of Ahrmehnee hospitality, since few of them—all hardened guzzlers and tough specimens in top physical condition—could take more than a full day of the "party," many only half that time . . . or less. And Milo began to understand a little better the things which he had found hard to fathom in years past—how parties of middle-aged or even older raiders could hike units of pursuing Regulars into the ground, then suddenly turn and assault the exhausted troops with all the savage ferocity of a treecat.

As he drifted off into a much-needed sleep on one of those nights—his ears still assailed by the wild, rhythmic music, still seeing in his mind's eye the bright bonfires and the circles of sinuously weaving women, the long lines of leaping, stamping, whirling warriors—he thought, "Hahfos and that Ahrmehnee girl will be a start. What a mixture *that* will be! Horseclans stock and Ehleen and now Ahrmehnee, and more than a few dashes of the Middle Kingdoms—in another hundred years, this Confederation should be home to an unbeatable race!"

EPILOGUE

Dr. Sternheimer had been admiring his fine new young body when his intercom buzzed. He strode quickly across his bedroom, reveling in the lack of those arthritic pains which his previous body had begun to develop, and depressed the button, looking up at the screen, but prudishly keeping his own nudity out of range of the video-camera.

"Doctor," announced the caller, "the Armenian Expedition is back at the Broomtown Base. Dr. Braun is on the radio now. I . . . I think perhaps you had best speak with him yourself, doctor."

Hurriedly, Sternheimer slipped into a coverall and zipped it while stepping into a pair of canvas shoes, left his suite and jogged down the hall to the lift, then changed his mind and took the stairs, three at a time. He arrived at the top of the seven flights sweating lightly, breathing normally and inordinately pleased at the overall fitness of this most recent body.

On the roof of the main tower, the shielding had been rolled back and a cool breeze with the tang of the sea brushed his face and ruffled his dark, wavy hair. As he began jogging toward the distant penthouse which was the communications center, the distant, booming roar of a bull alligator drew his gaze to the north.

Though the morning sun was already cresting the eastern horizon, its heat was not yet sufficient to dispel the misty fogs of the night and, as far as the dark-brown eyes of Sternheimer's latest body could see, the deadly swamps were covered in a billowy haze. The ocean of opaque whiteness was only marred by the upthrust tops of the taller trees—pine, cypress, swamp oak.

The bull boomed yet again. Closer to hand, a stooping eagle sank swiftly into the mists, then reemerged, broad wings beating for altitude. In its cruel claws some long animal writhed and jerked. Too short and broad, thought Sternheimer, to be a snake; most likely a large lizard then, or an immature crocodile. As he pressed his two thumbs to the identification plate of the door, he watched the avian hunter flap away westward with its catch.

"Braun? Sternheimer, here. How was your trip?"

The voice from the transmitter sounded weary unto death. "A bloody balls-up, David, from start to finish. Jay Corbett is dead, and Erica too, probably. Both my . . . this body's legs are becoming gangrenous, and I'm going to have to make a transfer soon."

"Were you able to get the devices out, Braun, and the precious metals?" Dr. Sternheimer snapped. He could not have cared less about his subordinate's physical ills: bodies, after all, were expendable.

Braun sighed deeply. "Oh, we got them out of that volcanic valley, David—over a hundred packloads, in all."

Sternheimer smiled broadly, admiring his expanse of even white teeth reflected up at him from the polished metal surface of the table. "What's the total tonnage, Braun? One of the cargo copters is down for maintenance, but I can send the other two up and—"

Braun sighed once more. "That won't be necessary, David. Those packloads and animals are scattered along two hundred miles of mountain trails, along with the corpses of the guards and packers."

The smile quickly disappeared. When Sternheimer spoke again, his voice was cold and tight, tight as the clenched teeth behind the almost immobile lips. "You had better start at the beginning, Dr. Braun."

"As you wish, David, as you wish. Corbett and I deduced that the volcano was on the verge of a major eruption, and he determined that if we could block the fissure that served it as a safety valve, we—"

"Yes, yes, I know all that, Braun. I approved it, remember?" Sternheimer found it difficult to keep the frustration and anger out of his voice.

"Well, David, we must have miscalculated somewhere along the line. The eruption was two days later and infinitely more violent than we had imagined it would be. We had forded the Catawba River and were skirting the northwestern flank of an odd rectangular plateau—making as rapid a progress as we could, since we were expecting a pursuit of some kind in the absence of an eruption—when a terrible earthquake occurred. We lost half the packtrain right there, David. A good half-mile of cliffs collapsed outward and buried them—men, mules, ponies, everything!

"The animals which survived went wild, of course—panicked, bolted, threw their riders or fell on them. That's what happened to my left leg; it was fractured and partly curshed when my mule fell. The mountain over the volcano must have literally exploded, because huge chunks of superheated rock fell all over the place. The piece of granite that landed on top of Corbett must have weighed all of twenty or thirty *tons*, David, and was still too hot to touch a day later.

"David, poor Erica was a brick, then. She reorganized our remaining men, set up camp right there on the spot and sent out patrols to round up as many of the animals as could be found. She set my leg, splinted and bandaged it and had a horse litter rigged up for me. It developed that we still had most of the devices, although almost all of the metals had been buried, as had our transceiver and all our extra weapons and ammunition.

"That night, it looked like the whole world was ablaze, with forest fires in every direction, as well as the continuing fireworks from that damned volcano. The only thing that saved us from being roasted alive was that Erica had had the forethought to burn off all the underbrush in the area, while the wind was being sucked northward in the immediate aftermath of the initial eruption. As it was, we had to shelter as best we could under rock overhangs and in crevices to escape the night-long falls of hot ash from the volcano and windborne embers from the fires."

Sternheimer's voice gave no indication that he was at all impressed by the tale of horrors. "All right, Braun, that's quite enough embroidery. Get down to the bottom line, man. Enormous expense and labor went into fitting out your expedition, and I want a damned good reason why it, and you, failed. How did you lose the devices?" He waited for a moment, then, "Well, Braun . . . Braun, are you there?"

Another voice came through the earphones, however. "Dr. Sternheimer, this is Mark Morton speaking. As medical officer for this installation, I must advise you that to interrogate Dr. Braun longer at this time will be to risk his total death. His present body is very near to expiration, all of its systems having been poisoned by the massive infections in its lower extremities. I have administered to him all the drugs I dare to; any more and he will lose consciousness, and he might not then regain consciousness enough to effect a transfer to a sound body."

"Oh, very well," snapped Sternheimer peevishly. "Let the fumbling fool make the transfer. I'll not deny him life. But put on the base commander now."

Saul Perlman sounded apologetic. "All I know, David, is that some friendlies rode into the base here, with Dr. Braun on a travois, having found him tied to the saddle of a dying mule. He was out of his head with pain and fever, and they only brought him to my base because the chief had recognized the mule as one of ours.

"The point at which the game hunters found him is well to the west of the planned route of return; therefore, surmising that—out of his head as he was—he might have strayed from the main party, I had one of the scout copters manned and we made two full-range sweeps to the north." He paused, then added, "We found what was left of them on the second. I've but just come back from there."

"And . . . ?" probed Sternheimer.

"Eighty kilometers almost due north of Broomtown and nearly seven kilometers west of the mapped route, they were apparently ambushed. From the conditions of the remaining bodies, I'd say they all died a week or ten days ago. We found the corpses of twenty-two men, nine mules and four ponies at what looked like the site of the ambush; all the human bodies had been stripped and hideously mutilated and every scrap of trappings and loads had been removed from the dead animals. The mules had all been skinned, David, and so"—he gagged and gulped— "had several of the men!"

"Now there's a practice I've never heard of," said Sternheimer.

"Neither had I," Perlman continued. "The tribes around here don't do such things, but I've heard traders speak of some tribe or tribes well north of here which are incredibly savage and bestial. Let's hope they're not migrating south."

"Any sign of Erica Arenstein?" demanded Sternheimer.

"None," replied Perlman. "And we searched very carefully, very thoroughly, for all that the stenches were almost unbearable in places. And from the little that poor Braun has been able to tell us, I think she was killed or captured sometime prior to that final fight.

"Somehow, Braun and at least two others got away. At least, we found two whole and clothed bodies of men who had been sent along as guards. One was about fifteen kilometers south; he and his animal had fallen into a gorge and we were lucky enough to spot them from a copter. The other was dragged in by some of the locals, and they were gone before we could question them."

"Think your 'friendlies' might have killed him?" inquired Sternheimer.

"No, the javelin head that Mark took out of his right lung was almost identical to the one he took out of Braun's leg—an entirely different pattern from the locally produced weapons. They were very crude, David, of iron, not steel, and wickedly barbed."

"Well, Braun can no doubt shed more light on this botched business," Sternheimer concluded. "As soon as his transfer is concluded, I want him brought down here to the Center. Were I at all superstitious, I'd have to think that there's a jinx on all our efforts against those damned mutants. Nothing has gone right for us, for our designs, since Moray led his horde of stinking nomads east from the Great Plains.

"Sometimes I wonder if we'll ever see the end of him."

About the Author

ROBERT ADAMS lives in Richmond, Virginia. Like the characters in his books, he is partial to fencing and fancy swordplay, hunting and riding, good food and drink. And when he is not hard at work on his next science fiction novel, Robert may be found slaving over a hot forge to make a new sword or busily reconstructing a historically accurate military costume.

⊘

SIGNET Science Fiction You'll Enjoy